BADGER IN THE BASEMENT

James was standing quite still, close to the sett. 'Shh . . . !' he said.

Mandy stood still and listened. She heard the wind gently sighing through the branches. Nothing else, except a small, miaouing sound.

James paused again, waited, and then bent to push aside the pile of loose earth with his hands. Mandy saw him gently lift something up out of the ground.

'What have you found?' she asked.

'Shh . . . !' James said again. But he turned and showed her what he was holding. It was small and helpless. It was a badger cub.

Animal Ark series

LUCY DANIELS

Badger
—in the—
Basement

Illustrations by Shelagh McNicholas

Hodder
Children's
Books

a division of Hodder Headline Limited

Special thanks to C. J. Hall, B.Vet.Med., MRCVS. for reviewing the veterinary information contained in this book.

Animal Ark is a trademark of Working Partners Ltd
Text copyright © 1994 Working Partners Ltd
Illustrations Copyright © Shelagh McNicholas 1994
Created by Working Partners Ltd, London W6 0QT
Original series created by Ben M. Baglio

First published in Great Britain
in 1994 by Hodder Children's Books

This edition published in 2001 by Hodder Children's Books

The right of Lucy Daniels to be identified as the Author of
the Work has been asserted by her in accordance with the
Copyright, Designs and Patents Act 1988.

For more information on Animal Ark, please contact
www.animalark.co.uk

35 34 33 32 31 30 29

A catalogue record for this book is available from the British Library

ISBN 0 340 60775 0

Typeset by Avon Dataset Ltd, Bidford-on-Avon B50 4JH

Printed and bound in Great Britain by
Clays Ltd, St Ives plc

Hodder Children's Books
a division of Hodder Headline Limited
338 Euston Road
London NW1 3BH

To Bette Paul

One

Mandy Hope sat watching her pet rabbits hopping across the lawn.

'Come on, come to me,' she called. 'Over here – come on!'

The two rabbits hopped towards her, stopping now and then to nibble the short, fine turf. They moved slowly towards her and Mandy made encouraging clicking noises at them. She smiled at them too, though her mother told her they couldn't recognise her smile. But Mandy always smiled at her rabbits just because they were her very own rabbits.

In a household where dozens of animals came

every day, Mandy took great pride in her own pets. Her adoptive parents were both vets; her home was Animal Ark, a surgery and hospital for sick and injured animals.

Mandy loved all of them, but it was good to have a couple of perfectly healthy creatures to herself. Still smiling, she put out a hand to lead them towards her, and clicked her tongue gently. For a moment they stopped and listened, quite still and alert, then slowly lolloped across the grass to her. It was so quiet in the garden that Mandy could almost hear their back paws thump the turf.

But just as they approached her hand, a louder thump sounded from the house. Startled, the rabbits scattered and Mandy heard her mother's voice cut across the garden.

'Mandy – have you got any homework?'

'Oh, Mum, you've disturbed the rabbits,' Mandy answered.

'Oh, I'm sorry, love. I wanted to catch you before you went down to your rabbits. Remember what Dad says – homework first, animals second! Pop them back in the run, now, please.'

That was easier said than done! The rabbits had scattered into the flower-beds so Mandy had a delightfully hectic race around the garden before they were safely gathered in.

'Here I am, Mum!' she called on her way through the kitchen.

'Oh, Mandy, just look at your shirt!'

Mandy looked down. She was wearing her favourite old denim shirt, rather dirty now after the rabbits had scrabbled all down it.

'Sorry, Mum. You did ask me to put the rabbits back in the run so I just picked them up from the flower-beds.' She looked sunnily up at her mother, knowing she'd be forgiven.

She was right. 'Oh well, if you want to wear that shirt tomorrow you'll have to wash it yourself; I'm off to yoga at the village hall right now.'

Mandy grinned. 'No, that's all right, I'll wear something else.' Mandy never did care what she wore, so long as she could discard her school clothes as soon as she arrived home. She watched her mother prepare for class.

Emily Hope was not much taller than her daughter, and, wearing black leggings and sweat-shirt, didn't look so very much older. Pulling her red curls up on top of her head, she leaned across and kissed her daughter.

' 'Bye, love. Dad's in surgery. I'll be back about eight. OK?'

'OK.' Mandy was used to being left in charge of the house. Theirs was an independent kind of family; both parents were very busy people, called out at all hours, running the surgery six days a week, with only Simon, the veterinary nurse, and Jean Knox, the receptionist, to assist them. And herself, of course; Mandy was always eager to help with the animals. Now, she happily waved her mother on.

' 'Bye, then, Mum – see you!'

One of Mandy's jobs was to sweep out the kennels and the animal hospital. So, with Mum safely out of the way, Mandy decided that was what she was going to do next. The homework could wait!

An hour later, Mandy had swept up, pausing only to stroke and soothe a few furry, fevered brows, as she always did straight after school. She couldn't always feed the animals; some were post-operative and would be sick, others were on special diets, but she loved coming in to see them every day to hand out lots of TLC, as Mr Hope sometimes called her treatments.

'A shot of penicillin, four hugs, five pats and half a kilo of Mandy's special Tender Loving Care,' he prescribed for any animal sick enough to have to stay in Animal Ark for a few days.

She'd just finished what she liked to think of as her 'round' when she heard her name being called again.

'Mandy! Mandy!' That certainly was not her mother this time. Mandy knew who it would be: Jean Knox, the surgery receptionist, in need of help, as usual. Jean was a warm, sympathetic receptionist but terribly absent-minded.

I'll bet she's lost yet another pen, Mandy thought as she opened the sliding door into the reception area. 'Can I help you, Jean?' she asked.

'Oh, Mandy, your father's so very busy just now.' The receptionist lowered her voice. 'That Pekinese, you know,' she almost whispered.

Mandy smiled at Jean's delicacy. 'That Pekinese' was in the middle of a difficult pregnancy and, as she was Mrs Ponsonby's pride and joy, she was at Animal Ark almost daily.

'So how can I help?' she asked, looking round. reception was empty at that hour.

'Outside, love – the man in that blue van; you can't miss it, it's blocking the entrance. But he won't come in, I've asked him. Will you go and take the details? I'm right in the middle of doing the records.' Jean peered at the computer screen and began to pick at the keyboard as if it would bite her.

Mandy was only too happy to postpone her homework. She took a pad and pen and went out to the carpark. She soon saw the old blue van parked across the entrance, but there was no sign of its owner. Puzzled, she went up and tapped on the van door. A sharp, narrow-faced man opened the window and leaned out.

'Yeah?' he asked, looking down at Mandy suspiciously.

'I've been sent to get your details.'

He looked surprised, then disgruntled. 'I've come to see the vet, not some kid.'

Mandy flushed. She was used to the clients worrying about her handling their pets, but they weren't usually so rude.

'Dad's busy just now,' she apologised. 'If you give me all the details, it'll save time later.'

She flipped her pad open and held her pencil ready, hoping she looked efficient, though it wasn't easy, peering upwards at the driver.

'Your name, please?' she asked, brightly.

'Bonser.'

Mandy was puzzled. 'Is that you, or the dog?' she asked.

'*Mr* Bonser,' he said. 'Old Dyke Farm. And the dog's just a dog; no fancy name. And no fancy hospital bill either, tell your dad. I'm not a rich man.'

Mandy leaned on the van door to write the notes on the pad. There were sprays of rust holes around the front wheel, she noticed, and the wing was badly dented. It was certainly a battered old vehicle. No wonder he was worried about the bill for his dog. Not that it would worry her dad: he'd treat the animal whether the man could afford it or not.

'Will you bring . . . er . . . your dog in now?' she asked.

'No, I won't,' he answered rudely. 'She won't let me move her. You'll have to get the vet out here.'

Mandy backed off and returned to Animal Ark. Luckily, Mr Hope was now free.

'That Pekinese, Pandora, will pay for our next holiday,' he greeted her. 'She's my best friend just now.'

'Well, there's a not-so-best-friend outside demanding you come and see his dog,' said Mandy.

Mr Hope finished scrubbing his hands. 'I'll be right out,' he said. 'And, Mandy . . .'

'Yes?'

'Remember, humans are animals too!'

Mandy often forgot that; she could handle just about any distressed animal, from sickly snakes to poorly parrots, but she was not always so understanding with their owners.

'People are sometimes rude when they're nervous,' Dad explained as they walked together to the carpark. 'Stress, you know.'

Mandy sighed. 'Well, I suppose he could just be worried,' she admitted. 'Even so, he *was* rude.'

Dad stopped and turned to face her, his dark eyes stern. 'I hope you weren't rude back?'

Mandy tipped back her head, shook her thick, blonde hair and looked up at him. 'No, I think I was quite polite,' she said, honestly.

'I'm sure you were, my love.' He grinned at her. 'And seething! Thanks for coping with him – let's go and see what we can do.'

Mandy almost wished she hadn't gone to see. The injured dog lay in the back of the van, on an old plastic sack. No basket, no box, just the half-conscious animal on the hard floor. Standing by her father's side, Mandy was tall enough to see the muddy, blood-stained creature, with a foxy, pointed face and shining, terrified eyes.

'Let's see, now, beauty...' Adam Hope leaned in and gently felt all over the creature, which snarled and snapped at him.

'Steady, now,' he murmured.

But the dog wasn't at all steady, and Mandy joined in with her father, making soothing sounds, calming it down.

'Fetch a blanket, Mandy, she's shivering with shock.' He shot an accusing glance at the owner, who didn't even notice. Mr Bonser stood back gloomily, whistling through his teeth, looking as sharp and foxy as his terrier.

When Mandy came back she noticed the cold silence between the two men. Her father must have had a taste of Mr Bonser's bad temper!

Expertly, Mr Hope wrapped the blanket like a sort of sling round the dog and gently lifted her out of the car. The little dog lifted her lip in a pathetic attempt to snarl.

'Come across to the surgery,' he said to Mr Bonser.

'I'm in a hurry,' he said. 'You just give me an estimate; I'll decide whether it's worth it.'

Mandy was horrified. The man spoke as if he'd brought his old van in to be mended, not a real live dog. She held her breath, waiting for Mr

Hope's sharp reply. But he'd already disappeared into Animal Ark, expecting them both to follow.

Mr Bonser made no move. 'Tell your dad to ring me later.' He turned back to the van. 'And tell him if the treatment's too dear he'll just have to get rid of the dog. Don't forget, now!'

He made a sudden dart into the vehicle, turned on the ignition, pressed hard on the accelerator and swept out of the carpark.

Mandy leapt out of the way and watched him pull out into the lane without stopping. He could have caused an accident, she thought indignantly. And she thought of his dog; somebody had

certainly caused an accident to happen to her. And Mr Bonser wasn't even prepared to pay for treatment! Mandy flushed with indignation at the idea. How could he say such a thing? Well, one thing was certain: the little dog would get the best treatment at Animal Ark, whether Mr Bonser agreed or not.

Mandy made her way indoors. In reception she paused, part of her longing to follow Mr Hope into the surgery, part of her accepting that he wouldn't let her in just then; she'd just get in his way. She sighed and turned back into the house. The homework was still waiting.

Two

' . . . and she hasn't even got a name, you know,' Mandy said indignantly. 'The poor little animal!'

James said nothing. He was peering through the misted-up window, looking as miserable as the weather. It had been raining hard that morning so they'd taken the bus to school and now they were on their way home, packed in amongst the damp Walton shoppers.

'You're not listening,' Mandy accused him. 'You haven't heard a word I've said.'

'What?' James shook his head. 'Sorry,' he muttered. 'I was watching the rain.'

'That won't stop it,' said Mandy.

'No,' he agreed, dolefully. 'And I was looking forward to the first outing of the Welford Wildlife Watchers. We're going up to Piper's Wood with Walter Pickard, badger watching.'

'You're going to get wet, then,' said Mandy. The Welford Wildlife Watchers had just been formed and James was a very keen member. Mandy wished she could join, too, but most of her time was taken up with the sick animals at Animal Ark. 'Listen, I was telling you about this dog that was brought in yesterday evening . . . '

She repeated the whole story, and this time James listened.

'But your dad'll treat the dog even if that man won't pay,' James said. 'He always does.'

Mandy knew this only too well. She'd sat through many a discussion at the kitchen table, listening to her parents trying to balance feed figures and drugs bills against unpaid accounts and their own sympathy for suffering animals.

'I know Dad won't let a healthy dog die if there's any chance of saving her,' she said, standing up as the bus came into Welford.

James moved down the empty bus after her. 'And is there a chance of saving her?' he asked.

Now Mandy's blue eyes were serious. 'He'll save

her,' she assured him. She jumped off the bus at the Fox and Goose and waited for James to join her. 'But what's the point of saving the poor animal and sending it back to that Mr Bonser if he's not even interested in her?' she asked angrily.

'Well, it is his dog,' said James, reasonably.

'But some people aren't fit to keep a dog,' Mandy sniffed, quite upset at the thought of Mr Bonser taking the dog back. ' 'Bye!' she called to James and she turned and walked quickly up the lane to Animal Ark.

Her first call was to the modern extension built at the back of the old cottage. It always amused Mandy that both her home and her parents' business was called Animal Ark. But she loved the idea of living in an ark full of animals. Ignoring the entrance to the cottage, she went round the side into reception.

'Hi, Simon!' she called. 'How is she today?'

The surgery nurse looked up from the desk, where he appeared to be putting a camera away. 'Pandora Ponsonby, you mean?' he teased.

'No, you know, the little terrier.' Torn between wanting the dog to be cured and not wanting to send her back to the unsympathetic Mr Bonser,

Mandy was not in the mood for teasing.

Simon was quick to understand. 'Come and see,' he said. He led her down the corridor to the little room where the dog lay.

'She's still sleeping a lot,' he told her. 'We've pinned the leg and stitched her chest. So long as there's no further infection she should pull through. Trouble is, she's not in good condition. Looks half-starved to me.'

Mandy wasn't squeamish; she peered closely at the sleeping animal. She could always cope with sick or injured creatures, clean them, hold them, mop up all kinds of unspeakable messes, but she hated to see them in pain. It was one of the things that worried her when she thought of becoming a vet.

She bent over the sleeping terrier and swallowed hard. The wounds went right round the little dog's chest, deep and curved though neatly stitched and clean, now. 'What could have happened to her?' she asked Simon.

He shrugged. 'Looks as if she was attacked.'

'But who would do that to a little terrier?' Mandy asked, horrified.

'What, not who,' Simon explained. 'Some kind of fight, I should think.'

'With another dog?'

Simon shook his head. 'I'm not sure,' he said. 'These wounds don't look like dog bites somehow.'

'A cat, perhaps?'

'It would have to be some special sort of cat!' said Simon. 'And I don't think we have panthers round Welford!'

Mandy looked thoughtfully at the sleeping terrier. 'Wasn't there some sort of wild cat reported, hiding in the woods last winter? People found tracks and sheep were attacked. Do you remember?'

Simon nodded. 'I remember the newspaper reports,' he said. 'But I think it was all a hoax. The only wild cat round here is Walter Pickard's Tom – you should try giving him an injection!'

'Well, whatever it was, it's left some odd-looking marks,' Mandy observed.

'Yes, I've been taking a few photographs for the records.'

Mandy took another peek at the patient. 'Is she unconscious?' she asked Simon.

'Just sleeping,' Simon assured her. 'I gave her a jab to make her drowsy; she mustn't move that leg just yet and she's a bit of a chewer so it's best to keep her sleeping.'

As if to defy Simon, the terrier shifted in her sleep and whimpered. A wash had revealed patches of white amongst the sleek brown coat, and a patch of white over one eye.

'Another Patch,' murmured Mandy. Patch was the name of a kitten Mandy had rescued and given to the Spry twins.

'Now, Mandy,' Simon warned her. 'That's not her real name.'

'She hasn't got a real name,' said Mandy, sadly.

'Well, it's not up to us to give her one. Come on, now, let's leave her in peace.'

He was right, of course, Mandy thought, as she followed him out. It was one of Dad's rules for Animal Ark that animals must be called by the name their owners gave them.

But Patch hasn't got a name, Mandy argued to herself as she went up to her room to change out of her school clothes. *She's got an owner and a home and yet she hasn't got a name*. How could someone keep a dog and never give it a name? It was very odd, even for Mr Bonser.

But Mandy had no more time to ponder on the mystery. She had her rabbits to feed and several sick animals to visit before supper, *and* a stack of homework after.

She was just finishing her history when James rang.

'Mandy, have you still got *Secondary Mathematics*, Book Two?' he asked, anxiously. 'I've just been promoted to it and I've left mine at school.'

Mandy grinned into the phone; James was excellent at maths, already a whole book ahead of his year. Luckily, she'd not yet finished Book Two herself.

'Don't tell me!' Mandy reached for her school-bag. 'I'll get Simon to drop mine in on his way past. All right?'

'Great – thanks . . . er . . . how's the dog?' James asked eagerly, just as Mandy was about to replace the receiver.

'Patch?' she said brightly. 'Oh, she's all right; a bit weak and sleepy.'

'Thought you said she hadn't got a name?'

'She hasn't, that's just my private name for her.'

In the silence that followed, Mandy could almost hear James's thoughts. He knew that Mr Hope was usually quite strict about not giving animals names. She waited for him to remind her.

But James merely coughed a little and said, 'The badger watch was called off after all.'

'Why? Were the Welford badgers too busy to

watch Welford Wildlifers?' she joked.

'You're nearly right. The badgers have disappeared from their sett in Piper's Wood.'

Mandy felt a sudden spurt of interest. 'Where to?' she asked.

'Who knows? I just got a message to say the meeting was called off. So I'll get on with the maths instead. Thanks again for the book.'

'OK – 'bye!' Mandy put down the phone and sat back. She was thinking furiously, and not about history. Somewhere at the back of her mind an idea stirred. What was it Simon had said about Patch's wounds? 'A special sort of cat!' And now, down in Piper's Wood, the badgers had gone. Why? Frightened off, perhaps, by the same cat that had attacked Patch?

'Have we got any books about badgers?' Mandy asked her dad over supper.

'Since when have you been interested in badgers?' he asked.

'Since now,' she grinned back at him. 'So where are the books?'

Mr Hope's study was lined with books and those that didn't fit on the shelves were piled in heaps on the floor. Mrs Hope often offered to sort them out for him, but her husband knew she was joking;

he couldn't bear anyone to disturb them. Meanwhile, only he could find anything in there.

Together, he and Mandy went across the stone-slabbed hall into the oldest corner of the cottage. Mandy loved the study, with its slightly musty smell of books and paper. It was a long, low room, with a thick single beam running the length of the ceiling. The bookshelves ran right along three walls, even up to the deep-set windows at the end where Grandad's big old desk stood. The desk was so big that Mandy could have walked across it, and often had done, when she was younger.

Mr Hope was browsing through a pile of papers on the desk. 'Ah, yes, here we are . . . I knew I'd seen an article about the local badgers recently.' He handed her a rather boring-looking magazine, small and tightly printed.

Mandy flipped through the pages. 'There aren't any pictures,' she complained.

'I thought it was information you wanted, not pretty pictures.'

'A bit of both, Dad, please.'

Mr Hope turned to a low shelf where big books were stacked flat in a pile. He cocked his head and muttered to himself as he checked the titles.

'Mmm . . . here we are: *British Mammals of the*

Night. That's got some amazing photographs.'

Mandy took the huge book. 'Thanks, Dad,' she said. 'I'll be very careful with it.'

'You thinking of joining Welford Wildlifers then?' asked her father, curiously.

'Just doing a bit of research,' said Mandy.

Next day the rain had cleared so Mandy cycled to the Fox and Goose crossroads to wait for James.

'Hi, did you get the maths done?' she asked.

'Yeah – easy,' he puffed.

'Good, that means you're free this evening.'

James nodded. 'Got something for me to do at Animal Ark?'

'I've got something for you to do in Piper's Wood.'

He glanced quickly at her. 'Why Piper's Wood?'

'I want you to show me where the badgers live.'

'But I told you, they've gone.'

'I know, but I just want to see where they used to live. OK?' Mandy trod hard on her pedals and spurted ahead. 'See you later!' she called back.

'Sooner!' James yelled. 'Watch out, here I come!'

They arrived at the back entrance to the school in a dead heat, which made up for their late start. And as she worked her way through the busy school day, Mandy was haunted by the thought of Piper's Wood. She had no idea what she would find there, only a feeling that she had to go. The photograph in *British Mammals of the Night* had clearly shown a large male badger, digging a hole at the foot of a tree. Digging with two strong, black paws which ended in a set of strong, sharp claws.

Mandy recalled her conversation with Simon about Patch's injuries and shuddered. Any cat who could frighten a fully-grown badger would have to be a supercat!

Three

Mandy leaned on her bike's handlebars, sniffing deeply. After the previous day's rain, the beech woods gave off a pungent, musky smell.

'Mmm . . . !' she breathed. She loved the smell of the trees; it reminded her of damp autumn walks. She stirred the leaf-mould with her feet.

'Mandy – are you coming?' James had already hidden his bike in the bushes and was waiting for her.

Mandy shook off her daydream, turned and shoved her bike deep into the bushes too. Time for business – whatever that was! She wasn't sure exactly why she wanted to see the badger sett –

after all, it was empty. But there was just that niggling thought that there might be something important there.

James was leading the way, pushing through brambles and bracken with confidence. Mandy followed cautiously in his wake. It was all right for James; he often went rambling about in the undergrowth. But she preferred the bridle-paths. At least you knew where to put your feet there, she thought, stumbling over a hidden root and pitching forward.

'Ow!' she yelled. And she fell on to James's back.

'Hey! Go steady!' he cried.

'I can't go at all, unless you get a move on,' Mandy pointed out. 'Go on then!'

But James didn't move. 'Hang on, I'm just checking our position,' he said.

'We're lost, aren't we?' Mandy joked.

'No, not lost. Not really . . .' James began to move on, rather slowly. 'There should be a clearing somewhere here.' He peered through his glasses at the tangled bushes.

Mandy, a head taller, stretched up and surveyed the scene. Straight in front lay more brambles leading into thick woods; no sign of a clearing there. She stood on tiptoe and looked all round.

'The clearing's that way.' She pointed over to the right. 'Look, where the sun's coming through.'

James stretched upwards but he still couldn't see above the brambles. 'You'd better lead the way,' he admitted.

Mandy stepped out firmly now, ignoring the prickles and tangles. Pressing ahead, she soon reached the edge of the clearing.

'Here it is!' she called, triumphantly. She turned to wave to James, lost her balance and fell backwards down a grassy bank.

'Enjoy your trip?' James joked as he helped her up.

'You might have warned me,' protested Mandy.

James looked about him. 'You found the right place though. The badger sett is under those big trees.' He set off across the clearing.

Mandy brushed herself down and followed, muttering to herself. 'I might have sprained my ankle, or even . . .'

She stopped when she saw James. He was standing quite still, looking at the remains of a sandbank as if he'd seen something quite nasty in there. As she got close, Mandy could see that his face was white and grim, his eyes shiny behind his glasses. Mandy followed his glance but saw nothing more than heaps of sandy earth.

'Looks as though someone's been digging,' she said, puzzled.

James nodded, turned away from her, sniffed hard then took off his glasses and rubbed them on his jeans. After a moment he replaced the glasses and looked again at the mess.

'But why?' asked Mandy. 'What were they digging for?'

James took a deep, shaky breath. 'Badgers,' he answered, and sat down suddenly on a tree-stump.

Mandy gazed at the earthy bank with horror. She'd read enough of her father's book to realise that not everyone shared James's enthusiasm for badgers. Some people regarded them as pests. And she remembered that her mum had pointed out a letter from Sam Western in the local paper only a few weeks ago. He was complaining about people who wanted to protect badgers and foxes – 'vermin', he called them – and he claimed that they spread diseases amongst farm animals and should be rooted out.

'So where are the badgers now?' she asked James.

He shrugged. 'If they're lucky they've run away.'

'And if not?'

'Dead,' he said in a flat tone. 'Some people will hunt anything that moves.' He wiped a hand across his cheek.

Mandy was silent. She knew that some wild creatures were a nuisance to farmers, who had to protect their crops and animals. Vermin had to be put down; it was one of the hard facts of the countryside. But there were right and wrong ways of doing it. This looked like a rather nasty way to her.

'How do they kill them?'

He didn't look at her. 'They sometimes use gas, or send dogs to sniff them out . . .' He couldn't go on.

But Mandy knew what he meant. She'd read reports in the local paper about badger digging. A dog was sent down into a sett to face a badger. When the men above heard the barking, they knew just where to dig to get the badger out. Sometimes the badger would attack the dog and the men would let them fight it out. It had said in the book that a full-grown badger could injure, or even kill the kind of small dog used in this 'sport'.

A tremor of excitement went through her. Suddenly she knew what had drawn her to this place. What if Patch had been one of those dogs? And what if Mr Bonser had found her lost in the woods and was going to let her try again?

She turned to ask James, but one look at his face stopped her. He was gazing round hopelessly, scrubbing at his glasses now and then, as if to clear them. Mandy waited for a moment before speaking.

'Maybe all the badgers got away,' she said, hopefully.

But he wouldn't be comforted. 'No chance,' he said. And he went on scuffing his shoe in the soft earth, sniffing hard.

Mandy swallowed hard; she couldn't speak. She knew James was very upset too, but he wouldn't want her to fuss. She sat down beside him, quietly wiping her eyes with a grimy hand and watching his foot moving to and fro across the tracks in the soil.

'Hey, stop a minute!' She peered down at his feet. 'Look at this!'

James's foot stopped moving. 'What is it?' he asked.

'Look!' said Mandy again. 'These are tracks.'

'So?' James wasn't impressed.

'Well, maybe the people who came to dig out

the badgers drove up in a car.'

'I'm sure they did. They wouldn't come on their bikes, would they?' said James.

Mandy felt she wanted to shake him but remembered how upset he was and tried to be patient. 'Well, I'm going to follow the tracks,' she said, and set off, hoping he would follow.

She didn't get very far; once away from the loose earth, the tracks disappeared, though the undergrowth was flattened down where the car had driven through. Disappointed, Mandy followed the tracks back to the sett, where they were quite clearly imprinted in the sandy loam. She knelt down to examine them closely. They were wide and rather squashed. Well, whatever the vehicle was, it was bigger than a car. She put her face almost on to the soil. The prints were not as sharp as she'd expected in such soft earth. Rather blurred, as if the tyres weren't very good . . .

Mandy stood up with a surge of excitement.

'James, come over here, I think I've found something,' she called.

James sighed and dragged himself up. 'It's no use, Mandy,' he said. 'There's no sign of badgers here, now.'

'Well, there are plenty of signs of humans,' said Mandy. She stood and waited for James to come and see.

But James wasn't even listening to her. He was standing quite still, close to the sett, head down, one hand held up. 'Shh . . . !' he said.

'But . . .'

'*Listen*!' he whispered.

Mandy stood still and listened. She heard the wind gently sighing through the branches, sounding like a distant sea. Nothing else, except . . . yes, a small, miaowing sound. Alarmed, she looked over to James.

James stood for a moment, almost sniffing the air, then crept forward, steadily, silently, towards the remains of the sett. Once there he paused again, waited, and then bent to push aside the pile of loose earth with his hands. Then he knelt down and started scrabbling through the earth, like a dog after a bone. Before she could go to help, Mandy saw him gently lift something up out of the ground.

'What have you found?' she asked, moving over to join him.

'Shh . . . !' James said again. But he turned and showed her what he was holding. It was small and

helpless. It was a badger cub.

Mandy moved forward; she could see the little creature cradled in James's arms, shuddering now and then, and whimpering as if it was having a bad dream. Its coat was pale, hardly grey at all, the stripes barely visible on his head, and its nose was still rounded, not sharp. Its claws were already growing, though, and tangled in James's sweater.

'Oh, poor thing, left behind all on his own,' said Mandy, her voice full of anxiety.

'Lucky for him,' said James, grimly. 'He must have got buried by a fall of earth so they missed him.'

They both looked down at the little badger. Even as they watched, he raised his short snout and pushed it hard against James's sweater.

'He's hungry,' said James. 'That's how they feed, pushing down into the ground for worms and insects.'

'Well, maybe you should put him back then,' said Mandy.

James shook his head. 'He might be hurt,' he said. 'And anyway, I think he's too young to survive on his own.'

Mandy looked at the badger. She looked at James. 'So what are you going to do?' she asked, although she knew the answer.

It took them much longer than usual to get from Piper's Wood back to Animal Ark. James had wrapped the badger up in his sweater and tied it by the sleeves over his handlebars, like a little hammock. The cub was half-starved and exhausted, so he kept quite still in his woolly prison. Even so, James decided to walk, pushing his bike with one hand and balancing his burden with the other. Mandy rode slowly ahead, frowning to herself, thinking of the reception they'd get back home.

'*You'd* better take the badger to Animal Ark,' she told James. 'There's more chance of keeping him then.' Mandy was just as keen as he was to help the little badger, but she knew there would be problems.

James merely nodded and smiled. He would have agreed to anything just then, so long as the cub was safe.

He'd no idea of the trouble he was causing, Mandy thought. Wild animals were always difficult to keep at Animal Ark. They brought their own infections and even caught new ones from the tame animals. They had to be kept quite separately,

Mr Hope was always very firm about that, and that caused more work for everybody.

Mandy cycled slowly on to Animal Ark, partly to keep pace with James but mostly because she knew they were headed for trouble. She glanced back and saw James puffing after her, clutching the bicycle saddle with one hand, steadying the badger's hammock with the other. *Poor James*, she thought. *I hope we're not in for a disappointment.*

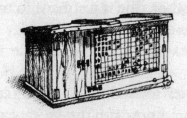

Four

'I'm sorry, but there it is,' Emily Hope spoke sadly. 'This is a veterinary practice, not a wildlife sanctuary.'

'But Dad's had wild creatures here before,' Mandy protested. 'Mr Bell brought that squirrel in after its mother was run over.'

'That's just the point, Mandy,' said her mother. 'Once that squirrel was treated, Ernie took it home; it wasn't at Animal Ark for long. But this little chap isn't even ill. He just needs a bit of food and shelter, and then what's going to happen to him?'

Mandy looked at James. He was holding the cub,

still swaddled in his sweater, and gazing ahead, blindly. Mandy could tell he was too upset to argue with her mother. She'd just have to try again.

'Mum, honestly, we'll do all the feeding. It'll be half-term next week and we'll be around all the time.'

Her mother looked at Mandy's pleading eyes and sighed. 'I know you'd take care of him,' she said, gently. 'And I'd love to give you the chance, but where will you put him? We simply can't risk putting a wild animal into the residential unit. One case of cross-infection and we'd lose our licence.' She put an arm round Mandy's shoulder and smiled sympathetically at James. 'I'll ring the wildlife sanctuary to see if they'll take him.'

At this, James woke up. 'But they're so overcrowded,' he protested. 'He doesn't want to go there.' And he clutched his bundle so hard that the badger squeaked.

Mrs Hope sighed. 'The sanctuary is busy just now, I know, but they do take good care of wild animals.'

Mandy looked at James's anxious face, then at her mother. 'Well, look, can we have a cage please, Mum?' she asked. 'Then at least we can make him comfortable for a while.'

Mrs Hope nodded. 'Of course,' she smiled. 'But make sure it's an old one; we may have to get rid of it later – and don't go into the surgery. There'll be a few old cages at the back of the garage.'

Mandy groaned; she knew when she was beaten. Mum was always reasonable, quite sympathetic – and very firm. She wouldn't give in. Sighing, Mandy led James across the yard.

Mr Hope was checking his emergency pack in the Land-rover. 'What have you got there?' he asked, seeing the bundle.

Mandy's heart sank as she watched James proudly presenting the little badger. Her dad looked very serious when they told him of their dilemma.

'Mum's right, you know,' he said. 'We can't risk infection – either for Pandora the peke or for this little chap.' He smiled and stroked the cub's snub nose gently.

'But he's got to have a home,' Mandy protested.

'First things first,' said her father. 'Let's see if we can find him a cage.' He looked under a shelf and came up with a rather battered travelling cage. 'Will this do?' he asked.

James looked doubtful, but even he realised that he couldn't keep the badger wrapped up in his sweater much longer. Mandy lined the cage with newspaper and filled it with straw. There was always plenty of both stored in the garage. James unrolled his sweater from the little cub and placed him gently down. The cub immediately began snuffling around and trying to nibble at the wire mesh.

'He needs food,' said James, looking worried.

Mr Hope reached into the Land-rover and took a packet from his box. 'This Vita-milk will keep him going for a while,' he said. 'We use it for bottle-feeding premature kittens and pups.' He peered closely into the cage and pushed a finger through the wire mesh. 'I think he's probably too old to suck . . . ow!' He cried and held out the finger. 'Yes, well, I asked for that, but at least it proves he's got his teeth! He'll manage a few pellets too. Mandy, you've got plenty of rabbit pellets – bring him a handful.'

They all stood round and watched as the badger lapped up the milk-mixture from a saucer and then snuffled through the straw after the pellets. When he'd finished he raised his little blue-and-white striped muzzle up to the bars of the cage, as if begging for more.

'What a little humbug!' murmured Mandy.

'What?' asked James.

'He doesn't belong to anyone, so let's call him Humbug,' said Mandy, smiling down into the cage.

But James still looked unhappy. 'It's not a name he needs, it's a home,' he said.

'What about your place?' suggested Mandy.

'My mum and dad won't allow wild animals in the house. They say that Blackie and the new kitten are quite enough for one house . . . and, anyway, there's nowhere for a badger to live at home,' he said. 'He needs a quiet, dark place for most of the day.'

Mr Hope nodded. 'Yes, of course he does, and a bigger cage with a separate sleeping area. Badgers are very particular about keeping their bedding clean.'

'We could make him a hutch,' said Mandy. 'Then he can go out on the lawn with my rabbits.'

'Not unless we want it digging over,' said her father. 'He may be a youngster but have you seen his claws?'

Mandy grinned. 'And then Grandad would be after him,' she said. 'Our lawn is his pride and joy. That's why he made me a new hutch . . .' She stopped, her eyes wide.

'So what did he do with the old one?' asked James.

'Put it in the basement back at Lilac Cottage.'

Mandy looked at James. He looked almost hopefully back at her. 'A basement's bound to be rather dark,' he said, thoughtfully.

'Come on!' commanded Mandy. 'I think a visit to my grandparents is in order!'

Mandy's grandfather was in his greenhouse, as usual.

'Hello, Mandy my love – and James. Come in – no, on second thoughts, there won't be room.' He came out to the driveway, shaking compost from his hands. 'Well, this is a nice surprise,' he smiled. 'Let's go into the kitchen and see if there's any tea.'

James looked frantically at Mandy. He couldn't bear to waste time having tea when his badger was still homeless. But he was too polite to say so.

Mandy understood. 'Well, actually, Grandad, we need your help first,' she said, and she told him all about finding the cub. 'So you see, we need that old rabbit hutch and a bit of space in your basement,' she finished.

Mr Hope looked thoughtful. 'Well, you can

certainly have the hutch,' he said. 'But as for letting a badger into our basement, well, you know what your gran is like!'

Mandy nodded; she knew her gran was devoted to Smoky, the kitten Mandy had given her, and *he* certainly wouldn't welcome a badger as a companion.

Still, first things first, Dad had said. 'Well, may we go and look for the hutch, Grandad?' she asked. 'We can talk to Gran about the basement later.'

She took James to the back of Lilac Cottage, down a set of steep, stone steps and into a dark, musty room below ground level. It had probably been a cold-store for milk, butter and cheese long ago, but now it housed the central heating boiler, garden tools long past their best, drying-out bulbs and rolls of spare carpet. It was warm and dry but too dark to be of much use; 'Tom's junk heap,' Gran called it.

Mandy pushed open the green wooden door and peered round in the dusky light. 'Hang on a minute, there's a light switch over the other side,' she said.

'No – wait,' James spoke urgently. 'This is just the right place for him, Mandy. It's dark and peaceful and warm, and we could look after him easily here. Do you think . . . ?'

'That Gran would let us use it?' Mandy sighed. 'Tell you what, James,' she said. 'Perhaps if we stay for tea we can persuade her.'

'Well, at least we can make him a comfy home,' said James. 'Where's that hutch?'

They soon found the hutch on a shelf by the boiler. It was quite clean and dry and Grandad came down and found old newspapers and wood shavings for the lining.

As they hunted for the shavings, Mandy explained to her grandfather that they wanted to make sure that the badger-diggers wouldn't come back to Piper's Wood.

'But how can you do that?' he asked.

'Well, there are tyre tracks all round the sett,' Mandy explained. 'They might prove who was there.'

Mr Hope nodded thoughtfully. 'You'll have to be quick off the mark,' he said. 'Tracks soon wash away if it rains. But don't you go hanging about the woods on your own, Mandy. Badger-diggers are not very pleasant folk.'

Mandy promised that she wouldn't do anything stupid. 'But you do see, don't, you, Grandad,' she said anxiously, 'why we've got to keep Humbug for a while?' Mandy and James waited for a reassuring reply.

But he merely suggested they all went upstairs to see whether Gran was home from her Women's Institute meeting at the village hall.

They found her in the kitchen, already getting tea. 'You'll stay and have some tea with us, won't you?' she beamed at them both. Mandy stared hard at James. This was their chance to persuade Gran to let them use the basement.

'Er . . . thank you, Mrs Hope,' he stammered. 'It's very kind of you.'

They hadn't realised how hungry they were. It was hours since school dinner and Mandy had been in such a hurry to get to Piper's Wood that they hadn't even stopped for a snack. Now they were able to do full justice to Gran's toasted teacakes and her gorgeous sticky parkin, all dense and dark and gingery.

Mrs Hope kept the inside of Lilac Cottage as beautifully clean and neat as Grandad did the outside. Which made the question of keeping a badger in the basement even more difficult. As she chatted on, Mandy could feel James's eyes on her; he was desperate to get away but even more desperate to find a home for Humbug.

'Well, thanks, Gran, that was lovely,' Mandy said, over-enthusiastically, as she stood to leave. When she didn't actually move to the door, her grandmother looked at her quizzically.

'Is there something you want, Mandy, dear?' she asked.

'What? Er, well . . .' For once, Mandy didn't know how to begin. She'd already told Gran about their trip to the woods and about finding the cub but hadn't mentioned the problem of a home for him. She had hoped that Grandad would come to her rescue, but he only talked to James about giving the old rabbit hutch a fresh coat of paint.

Now, three pairs of eyes rested on Mandy, Gran's puzzled, James's desperate, and Grandad's twinkling with amusement.

'You see, Gran, it's Humbug . . .' And as soon as she said his name, Mandy was off. She told her grandmother about the badger-diggers and Humbug's missing family, about the health and safety rules at Animal Ark, and about the lack of space at James's house. It was all Mrs Hope could do to stop the flow.

'So where do I come into all this?' she asked, with a little smile. And Mandy knew that Gran knew what they were going to ask. But to her surprise, it was James who spoke.

'Mrs Hope,' he said, very quietly, 'your basement is just the place for Humbug. He needs a quiet, dark, warm home, where he can get strong and healthy, before he goes back to the woods. Please would you let him stay in the basement – just for a while?' James turned bright pink and looked down at the table.

There was a pause so silent that they could hear the sparrows chattering outside.

Then: 'Well, I don't like the idea of a wild animal in the house. It might upset Smoky,' said Gran. 'But, after such a nice, polite request, how can I refuse?'

'Oh, thank you, Gran, thank you!' Mandy was back at the table, hugging and kissing her grandmother. Mr Hope was beaming at them both. James was already on his feet.

'I'll go and fetch him,' he said. 'And thank you very much, Mrs Hope.'

'Hey – wait for me. I want to carry Humbug back to his new home too,' laughed Mandy.

They ran down the lane back to Animal Ark, where they told Mandy's mother not to bother with the animal sanctuary and James rang his parents to tell them he'd be late. Then, together

they carried Humbug in the travelling cage, back up the lane to his new home in Lilac Cottage.

James lifted the sleeping badger out of his cage and settled him into the straw in the old rabbit hutch. Humbug merely stirred, snuggled into his new bed and slept on.

'Well,' said Gran, quite satisfied that the little creature was in no position to terrorise Smoky, 'we often have a hedgehog in the greenhouse and even moles in the lawn, but it's the first time we've had a badger in the basement!'

Five

On the first day of the half-term holiday, Mandy woke early. She opened her bedroom window wide and leaned dreamily on the sill, looking out over Animal Ark. She could hear the familiar sounds of hens from a nearby farm, and the cows murmuring as they came down from the meadow to be milked.

Mandy breathed deeply; the air was mild and damp, the clouded sky pearl grey. It would rain soon, she thought. And suddenly she was wide awake. Grandad had warned her that the tracks round the badger sett would be washed away by rain. If she wanted to get her evidence, she'd have to get moving!

* * *

'May I borrow your camera, Dad?' Mandy asked at breakfast.

'Hmm? Pass the marmalade, please.' Mr Hope was deep in thought, planning the day's calls.

'Dad! The camera – may I borrow it, please?' Mandy repeated slowly and loudly. 'And you've given up marmalade,' she reminded him.

Adam Hope groaned; he was always trying to lose weight. 'You can have the camera if I can have the marmalade,' he bargained.

Emily Hope laughed at the two of them. 'Well, that won't do either of you any good,' she said. She turned to Mandy. 'There's no film in the camera,' she explained. 'I can get you one in town later on today.'

Mandy sighed; one of the disadvantages of living in the country was the lack of shops. The McFarlanes kept their shop and post office stocked with everything from Coke to beefburgers but they didn't sell films. And by the time Mrs Hope got back from town, the rain would surely have started. So that was the end of that little plan, Mandy thought.

Her mind was already working on plan number two – James. She stood up and pushed her chair back sharply. 'I have to go – there's Humbug to see to.' And she shot out before anyone could protest.

James was already in the basement when Mandy arrived. Humbug was scurrying about in his travelling cage whilst James cleaned the hutch. Mandy filled up the bowl with rabbit pellets and took the feeding-bottle out of the wire mesh at the front of the hutch. Simon had advised them to use a bottle because badgers hate mess in their cages and Humbug was a very sloppy drinker!

'I'll hold Humbug while he drinks his Vita-milk,' she said.

James pushed his glasses up on his nose and looked through them at Mandy, very seriously. 'I've been talking to Walter Pickard,' he said. 'He says we mustn't play with the badger, or even pick him up.'

'Why not?'

'It'll muddle him.' James explained. 'We don't want him to be friendly with humans when he goes back home to the woods.' James looked anxious. 'We'll have to find a new sett for him,' he said. 'Somewhere far away from Piper's Wood.'

'Why?' asked Mandy.

'Well, I've been thinking,' said James. 'You know

whose land borders Piper's Wood?'

'No, whose?'

'Sam Western's!' said James.

And Mandy knew exactly what he meant. Sam Western would use any method possible to keep his land free of what he called 'vermin'. They both knew he'd tried to poison one of Lydia Fawcett's goats when it trespassed on his property. He was quite capable of flushing out badgers. But how? Mandy wondered. What about the tyre marks? To Mandy they looked quite worn and Sam Western would never leave worn tyres on his van. Unless he didn't want it known that he was in the woods and he used someone else's van?

Mandy looked at Humbug, then at James's tense face. This was just the right moment to tell him of her plan.

'Well, there may be something we can do,' she said slowly. 'You remember those tracks in the loose soil up in the woods?'

James nodded.

'Well, if we could trace the vehicle that made them . . .'

'But they could have come from anybody's van,' said James.

'Not these tyres,' Mandy assured him. 'They're

quite worn in parts. It should be easy to recognise them.'

'There must be lots of farmers riding around on worn tyres,' James pointed out.

'But not always in the same pattern,' replied Mandy. 'If we did some drawings of the tracks, we can keep a check on all the vans around here.'

James shook his head. 'We could never draw them accurately enough,' he said. 'And anyway, I can't come out this afternoon. We've got a family gathering – aunts and uncles to tea and all that. I've promised to show my cousin how to use his new computer game.'

He opened the travelling cage and tipped Humbug back into his hutch. The little badger snuffled round for his pellets and sat scrunching happily. Mandy watched him, gloomily. Plan number two dismissed! Sighing, she filled the bottle with the vitamin-milk powder and shook it up to mix it.

'Takes a bit of mixing,' she explained. 'You have to give it a good shake or the powder separates and it all goes chalky.' She held up the bottle in the dim light.

James watched her shaking the mixture.

'Plaster!' he said suddenly. 'That's what you need.'

'What?'

'To make plaster casts of the tracks in the wood.'

Mandy still looked puzzled so James explained. 'It's a way of checking animal tracks; we did it in environmental studies in the junior school. You make a mix of plaster of Paris, press it over the tracks, let it set, pull it off and, there you are, a perfect imprint!'

Mandy beamed. 'James, you're a genius!' she cried. 'We can go straight up there now. We'll need water – I can bring that in the bottle on my bike. You go and get the powder . . .'

'Where from?'

'Well, haven't you got some?'

'No, I told you – it was way back, when I was in the junior school . . .'

'Oh, James, what shall we do? We must get some sort of record of those tracks today; if it rains they'll all be washed away and we'll lose our evidence.'

They stood, deep in thought. Only the sound of the little badger, grinding at the mesh on his cage, disturbed the silence. James picked up the feeding-bottle, pushed it through the mesh and fixed it with a couple of rubber bands. Humbug stretched his neck and started to suck the tube at the end of the bottle.

'Oh, isn't he cute?' exclaimed Mandy. 'Mum says she'll call and give him a check-up later on. She'll be too busy just now: surgery's always packed on Saturday mornings . . .'

She broke off and looked at James.

'The surgery – of course!' she exclaimed. 'My parents sometimes use plaster to set broken limbs. I bet I can find some plaster of Paris at home.' Mandy turned to go. 'I'll fetch some then get straight off to Piper's Wood.'

'Hang on!' James hesitated. It was never easy to tell Mandy she couldn't do something. 'It's a bit tricky,' he said. 'My first few casts were useless; I didn't use enough powder.'

'So, what's the recipe?' Mandy pulled a chewed up Biro from her jeans pocket and prepared to write on her hand.

'I don't really know. I think a lot depends on the dampness in the air and on the state of the earth . . .' James sighed, heavily, trying to remember the details.

Mandy groaned. It all sounded very complicated and she was getting impatient.

'Tell you what,' said James. 'If you can be up at

the sett in half an hour I'll meet you there. But we'll have to be quick; Mum'll want me back for lunch – all those visitors, you know.'

Mandy grinned sympathetically. 'I'll be there,' she promised. 'Complete with plaster cast kit!'

'Plaster of Paris? What on earth for?' Mr Hope asked.

Mandy hesitated. She didn't want to tell lies to her father but, on the other hand, if she told him that she was on the track of catching a badger-killer he'd certainly forbid it.

'Er . . . I'm going to help James make plaster casts of some tracks,' she said, perfectly truthfully.

Her father laughed. 'You? You're not usually keen on tracking. What's come over you?'

Mandy, who couldn't think of an explanation right then, blushed and shook her head.

'It's not tracking I'm interested in, it's badgers,' she said. 'Since we got Humbug, you know . . .'

Well, that was certainly true!

'Go on.' Mr Hope grinned and ruffled her short blonde hair gently. 'The plaster powder's in the office. Help yourself to a small pack.'

'Oh, thanks, Dad!' Mandy leapt up to hug him and shot out of the door, almost knocking over her mother as she passed. 'Sorry, Mum – in a hurry!'

And she was gone.

Mandy pushed hard on her pedals; it was tough going uphill on the bridle-path through the woods but quicker than scrambling through the undergrowth like last time. She hoped James had managed to get away. What would she do if he hadn't? Well, she knew the answer to that; she'd just have to get on with the job all on her own.

But as she turned off the track into the clearing James's dog, Blackie, came bounding up to greet her.

'Hello, boy!' she said, dismounting before he could knock her off her bike. 'Have you brought James out for a walk?'

'Only a quick one!' came James's answer. 'Have you brought all the stuff?'

Mandy nodded. 'I even borrowed a plastic bowl to mix it in.'

'Great. Let's get on, then. I've found a few good ones close to the sett.'

The next few minutes were exciting. Mandy mixed the powder and water to a smooth, thick paste and watched with interest as James pressed it gently into the best of the tracks. After that, there was nothing more to do except to wait – and to keep Blackie from treading in the stuff!

Eventually, James looked at his watch. 'Twenty minutes – we'll have to risk it; I'm due home any time now.' He bent to peer at the plaster and tested it with his finger. 'This one's just about ready,' he announced. 'Did you bring anything to wrap them in?'

Mandy dived into her cycle bag and triumphantly waved a clutch of plastic bags she'd noticed hanging in the barn. James carefully lifted the first cast and placed it on the plastic bag.

'Leave it to dry a bit longer,' he told Mandy. 'I'll get the other two.'

He moved a bit further off and Mandy sat guarding the finished cast. She was so busy admiring it that she didn't notice Blackie running back and forth to the bridle-path, whining. It was only when he broke into fierce barks that she looked up.

There was a man standing at the edge of the clearing, watching them. Mandy picked up the plaster cast, thrust it into the bag and pushed it behind her. Then she stood up and called Blackie to heel. The man moved forwards a step or two. Blackie growled gently.

'He's quite a guard dog,' the man said. Now that he was closer, Mandy could see his face was ruddy, as if he spent a lot of time outdoors, and he had a short, grizzled beard. He was wearing a green body-warmer and a battered tweedy hat. 'What's he up to?' he demanded, nodding in the direction of James.

'He's . . . er . . . collecting,' said Mandy, thinking furiously. 'Tracks,' she added. 'They say there are badgers round here, you know,' she went on, brightly.

'Not any more there aren't.'

Mandy thought he sounded pleased about that. 'He thought he might pick up some prints.' She smiled nervously, praying that James would hear them talking and hide his casts. For all they knew this man might be one of the badger-diggers himself! As if to share her suspicions, Blackie gave another growl.

'Lovely dog, that,' the man said. But he didn't move any closer. 'Is he yours?'

'No. He belongs to James – over there.'

The man nodded. 'You want to watch him in these 'ere woods. Friend of mine lost a dog round here only a few days ago.'

'Lost a dog? How awful!' Mandy said. It was bad enough to have an animal die, but to lose one was even worse. You could never know what had happened to it. Mandy shivered at the thought of anything like that happening to Blackie.

She turned to look at the man who coughed gruffly and continued to stare at Blackie. Nervously, Mandy looked on. He had a friend who'd lost a dog, he said. And he seemed to know that the badgers had gone. What if he and his friend had lost the dog when they were looking for badgers? Digging for badgers?

'Hey, Mandy, can you bring me a bag, please?'

James's voice interrupted her speculations. And for once, Mandy was grateful.

'I'll have to go and help him now,' said Mandy. ' 'Bye!' She called Blackie and went quickly over to James.

'Shove those casts in the bag and hide them!' she commanded as soon as she was within earshot.

'No, leave them out to dry a bit longer. I'll have to get back but you can wait another ten minutes, just to make sure.'

'Just put them in the bag!' Mandy repeated. 'And give them to me!'

James looked up at her. 'What's the matter?' he asked.

'Over there – near the bridle-path,' Mandy jerked her head in the direction of the man.

James stood up and looked across the clearing. 'What?' he asked.

'That man – can't you see? He might be one of the diggers.' Mandy turned to look once more. The man had gone. And she remembered her promise to her grandfather. She wasn't going to linger in the woods on her own.

'Come on, we'll have to risk the plaster being dry. I'll pack them very carefully into my saddle-bag and dry them out at home.'

'But there's nobody there, Mandy.'

'There was; I spoke to him and he was very interested in what you were doing. I let him think you were collecting badger tracks. And he knew the badgers had gone.'

'Half the county knows that now. That doesn't make him a criminal,' said James.

'Whatever he is, I don't want to be left in the woods on my own with him around,' said Mandy. 'Now, come on, help me pack my bag, then you can get back to your cousin's computer game!'

Mandy rode back slowly and carefully, steering round all the stomach-jerking bumps she usually enjoyed. When she got back to Animal Ark, she took her treasures up to her room and set them out in the sun on the windowsill. Then she went in search of lunch.

'Had an instructive morning with James?' Mr Hope enquired. 'Soup and salad do you? We'll cook tonight when Mum's back from town.' He poured Mrs Hope's best home-made leek and potato soup into two bowls, fetched garlic bread from the oven and sat with Mandy at the kitchen table.

'Did you get some good tracks?' he asked,

watching longingly as Mandy spread butter thickly over her bread.

Mandy smiled and passed him a packet of crispbreads, but not the butter. 'Oh, yes, Dad,' she said. 'We got some terrific tracks!'

Six

'Shall I hold him while you clean out the cage?' Mandy asked James. It was a few days after they'd rescued Humbug and she was longing to have a chance to touch him and examine him closely.

'Nay, lass, you mustn't do that!' Walter Pickard had come to Lilac Cottage to see how the little badger was getting along. 'He's got to go back into the woods, d'you see. You don't want to make a pet of him.'

Mandy sighed, though she knew he was right; Walter Pickard was the village expert on wildlife and he'd given them some very useful advice.

'You're doing very nicely with the little 'un,' he

told them today. 'Coming on a treat, he is. You're giving him a good mixed diet, like I told you?'

'Oh yes, Mr Pickard,' James assured him. Walter had told them that even very young badgers like a bit of meat as well as their mother's milk. So every morning now they fed the cub on rabbit pellets mixed with raw mince.

'And you're keeping him nice and clean, I see.' Walter peered into the hutch and nodded his approval. 'Badgers do like to keep their places clean, you know.'

Mandy and James cleaned out the hutch, filled up his water bottle and then walked down the lane with Walter, leaving Humbug quite alone in the dark, peaceful basement. And although Mandy knew that was the right thing to do, it didn't stop her wanting to make friends with the little badger.

'Shall I take Patch for a little run while you clean out the kennel?' she asked Simon, later that same morning. They were standing in front of the terrier's kennel. 'She's getting better every day now.'

She was right; Patch's wounds had almost healed, leaving only faint stitch marks, and she trotted around quite confidently on three legs and a plaster. She was in an outdoor kennel, which was not a kennel at all, more a concrete run, completely enclosed in strong wire mesh and with a warm, cosy hut at one end. Patch was quite happy there, with enough room to move around, lots of good food and a comfortable bed in the hut.

'An outing will do her good now that she's moving so well,' Mandy said.

Simon shook his head. 'She's not your dog, Mandy. You can't go taking other people's dogs out without their permission.'

'But she needs the exercise.'

'She's getting quite enough at the moment, with her leg in plaster.' Simon moved on to the next run where a huge Great Dane was sprawled, looking very sorry for himself.

'Would you like to help me feed this one?' he asked.

But Mandy shook her head; it was Patch she wanted and if Simon wouldn't let her take the dog out, she'd take a mug of coffee to her mother and try to persuade her.

She found her in the office, sorting out Jean's muddles. 'Thanks, love, I'm ready for this.' Mrs Hope took the coffee and went on checking the appointments schedule.

But Mandy perched on the edge of the desk. 'Mum, you know that terrier?'

'Hmm?' Mrs Hope didn't raise her head.

But Mandy went on, 'Well, she's a lot better now, so I think I ought to take her out to exercise that leg.'

Mrs Hope looked up and reached for her coffee. She sipped it, slowly, smiling at Mandy over the rim of the mug. 'Yes, well, I think you're right,' she agreed.

Mandy beamed. 'You do? Then can you please tell Simon to let me take her out.'

'No, wait! I mean you're right about the dog being ready to move. She's not fully recovered yet, but there's no need for her to stay here, so long as Mr Bonser is careful with her.' She shuffled through some computer print-outs in front of her. 'Oh dear, Jean's not got the bill ready so I can't send it out. I'll have a talk to him when he comes in. He can only take the dog home if he understands how to treat her.' Mrs Hope picked up the internal phone. 'Jean? Can you pop in here a moment?' She looked at Mandy, expecting her to leave.

Mandy wandered back to the house, appalled. What had she done? Got Patch sent home, that's what. She frowned at the idea. Would Mr Bonser take care of Patch properly? He didn't even take care of his own van properly – it was worse than Simon's. And Mandy wasn't at all sure he'd listen to her mother's advice, as he'd been so rude on his previous visit to Animal Ark.

She recollected her father's words on that occasion: 'People are sometimes rude when they're nervous.' Perhaps if she went to see Mr Bonser on his home ground, he wouldn't be so nervous; perhaps he'd listen to her and she could make sure he'd treat Patch properly.

Mandy rushed off upstairs. Half-term wasn't going to be so dull after all! She knew Mr Bonser's farm; after all she'd filled in his card that day. Old Dyke Farm was a pig farm out towards the Beacon – on the way to Upper Welford Hall, where Sam Western lived.

As she pedalled off down the lane, Mandy suddenly thought of James. He always enjoyed a bike ride and he might even be useful back-up if Mr Bonser wouldn't listen to her. Mandy clicked up a gear and raced down the hill to James's house.

But James's delight in being invited to go for a bike ride soon turned to doubt when he discovered where they were going. 'You said he was rude and a bit rough,' he objected.

'Well, that might have been because he was worried,' explained Mandy. 'People sometimes sound cross when they're really just frightened,' she added, sounding more certain than she felt.

'But what if he's not even there?' said James.

'Oh, we'll just cycle up and look round. If anybody stops us we'll say we have a message for Mr Bonser – which we have.'

James couldn't deny this so together they cycled out of the village and up the hill. The main road was smooth and lovely to ride, but the narrow, twisty drive up to Mr Bonser's pig farm was in a poor condition; they bumped and banged up it, twisting and turning to avoid the worst potholes.

'If I get a puncture you can jolly well mend it,' said James, puffing and complaining all the way.

'All right – I promise!' Mandy herself was beginning to have doubts.

'Don't suppose you even have a repair kit in your bag,' James went on grumbling. Suddenly he dropped into a deep hole. 'Ow!' He stalled and fell off his bike.

Mandy stopped and dismounted in case he needed any help. But she suddenly heard the sound of a car engine. It was coming down the drive towards them.

'Quick, get up!' Mandy dropped her bike down into the ditch and rushed over to pick up James and push him to safety on the overgrown grass verge. Mandy peered through the long grass and saw that Mr Bonser was driving the van.

'Oh, no. He's gone out now,' she said.

'Good – we can go home.' James scrambled up and brushed himself down.

'Wait a minute, this is a good chance to have a look round the farm,' said Mandy.

'What for?'

Mandy hesitated; she had no idea but she didn't like to think they'd come all that way for nothing.

'You never know,' she said mysteriously. 'We might find out something about Mr Bonser.'

'I'm not cycling over those potholes again,' said James.

'OK, we'll walk.' And Mandy set off, leaving her bike hidden in the ditch. She knew that James would either wait for her or follow.

He followed.

Old Dyke Farm wasn't so much a farm as a sort of scrap-heap-cum-smallholding. Scattered about the yard in front of the small cottage were rusting machine parts, loose heaps of straw, piles of old motor tyres, lengths of timber, doors, even an old lavatory.

'What a mess!' said Mandy, surveying the scene.

'Being untidy's not a crime,' grinned James.

'No, but it's a funny sort of pig farm,' Mandy observed. 'I see no pigs!'

James sniffed. 'Nor smell any, either,' he said.

'Maybe he's gone bust?' They both knew that some local farmers were having a very difficult time just now.

Mandy frowned. 'Well, if he has he might be looking for new ways of making money. Come on, we might just find out what he's up to.'

'But what are we looking for?' asked James.

'I don't know – anything unusual – like a pig farm with no pigs.'

They went over to the piggeries, old concrete buildings now stripped and empty but securely locked, nevertheless. Mandy pulled at the first door but it wouldn't budge.

'There's nothing here, Mandy. Come on, let's go,' James said nervously. 'We shouldn't be poking about on somebody else's farm like this.'

'Oh, all right!' Mandy followed him along the

length of the piggeries, banging on each door as she passed.

At the last door she stopped. There was a faint sound coming from inside the sty. A sound of . . . whining, whimpering perhaps?

'There you are!' said Mandy, triumphant. 'Listen to that!'

They stood silent, listening hard. It certainly was a whimper, and a very faint, high-pitched squeaking.

'Pigs don't whimper,' said James. 'They squeal.'

'That's not pigs, it's dogs,' whispered Mandy.

'Oh, well, just the farm dogs, I expect.' James moved off.

'But they're locked in there – in the dark!' Mandy rushed after him. 'We can't leave them like that!'

James turned to her. 'Look, Mandy, plenty of farmers keep their dogs outside, in kennels, barns – boxes, for all I know. Mr Bonser will probably let them out when he comes back.'

'But if they're farm dogs he'd have left them on guard,' Mandy argued. 'They were crying to be let out – and to be fed, if I'm not mistaken. They sounded hungry, James!'

But James wouldn't even stop to answer; he was

anxious to get off Mr Bonser's land. Mandy gave a worried glance back at the piggeries, hesitated, then raced to catch up with James. Silently, they picked up their bikes and pushed them to the end of Mr Bonser's drive. They were just coming up to the main road when the ramshackle blue van turned in to the drive.

'Oh, help, it's him!' James moaned.

'Good!' Mandy was quite excited. 'Now, I'll do the talking while you get the registration number – OK?'

'But . . .'

Too late, James saw the van slow down and pull alongside Mandy, who was actually waving it down!

'Hi, Mr Bonser,' Mandy called cheerfully.

He slid back his window and peered down at her. 'What are you doing on my land?' he demanded.

Mandy waggled a hand behind her back to indicate that James should stay behind the van. 'Er . . . You are Mr Bonser, aren't you?' she asked, playing for time.

'Who wants to know?' he asked suspiciously. 'If you kids have been up to any mischief on my land I'll . . .'

'Oh, no, we just came to . . . to deliver a message, and you weren't there, so we were just leaving.'

'Message? Who from?' Mr Bonser suddenly looked anxious.

'From the vet – at Animal Ark,' Mandy explained. 'Remember me, Mr Bonser? I was there when you brought your dog in.'

Mr Bonser shook his head. 'My dog's here with me,' he said, jerking his head towards the back of the van.

Is it? thought Mandy. Then what were the other dogs doing, all shut up in a piggery? And who did Patch belong to? She glanced down and saw James, kneeling on the ground, peering at the battered number plate.

'Your injured terrier,' she reminded Mr Bonser. 'You brought her to Animal Ark.'

Mr Bonser seemed uneasy. 'Not my dog,' he said. 'Brought it in for somebody else.'

For a moment, Mandy was flooded with relief. Perhaps Patch wouldn't have to go back to Old Dyke Farm after all. 'Well, perhaps you could tell the owner his dog's nearly better.'

'And you've come all this way just to tell me that?' He glared at her in disbelief.

Mandy swallowed hard. 'Not just that, no. Er,

well . . . Mum says can you come and collect him,' she said, faintly, feeling terrible at betraying poor Patch. But she had to say something to explain her presence at Old Dyke Farm and the kind of heart-to-heart chat she'd planned didn't seem to be working. 'We need the kennel, you see, for another patient.'

Mr Bonser eyed her suspiciously. 'Oh, aye? And does your mum say who's going to foot the bill?'

Out of the corner of her eye, Mandy saw James getting up. 'Er . . . well, I suppose you'll have to discuss that with her,' she said, hurriedly. 'I must get back, now, I'll tell her I saw you. 'Bye!'

They leapt on to their bikes and pedalled hard without saying a word. When they reached the Fox and Goose crossroads they stopped, dropped their bikes on to the village green and flopped down on the bench beside them.

'Well – did you get the number?' Mandy asked.

James nodded. 'But what's it for?' he asked.

'I don't know,' Mandy admitted. 'I just thought it might be useful.' A thought struck her. 'Did you get a look at his tyres?' she asked.

He shook his head. 'Not specially,' he said. 'Why?'

Mandy shrugged. 'I just wondered whether

they'd match our plaster casts.'

'Well, I did notice the back tyres are very worn,' James admitted, cautiously. 'But that's as far as it goes.'

Mandy refused to be put down. 'So, we'll take it just a bit further,' she said.

'How?'

'Easy! Next time we see Mr Bonser's van we'll check his tyres against our casts.'

'Oh yeah? Like when? I've never seen him around Welford.'

Mandy bit hard on a grass stalk and turned away from James. 'He's got to come to Animal Ark to collect Patch,' she said. 'And he's bound to make trouble about the bill. While the discussion goes on, I can check his tyres against the casts.'

'I thought you didn't want the dog to go back to Mr Bonser?' James said.

Mandy sniffed. 'He might not get her back if we can prove he was involved in the badger-digging.'

They were both quiet for a moment. Mandy was weighing up the odds against Mr Bonser being caught and Patch being rescued.

'He might not come down to get the dog,' James said suddenly.

'Oh yes he will; Mum's sending for him.'

'But he might turn up when you're not there,' James pointed out.

He was right; they'd be back at school next week. There must be another way . . .

'Simon!' she said suddenly.

'Where?' James looked round.

'No – Simon's at Animal Ark most of the time; he can do it.'

'Do you think he will?'

'He will if you tell him about the badger-digging; he's a wildlife nut like you.'

James stood and drew himself up as tall as he could. 'The word is "enthusiast", not "nut", Mandy. You know sometimes I wonder why I'm your friend!'

Mandy grinned. 'Because you're a wildlife enthusiast!' she said. 'Now, let's go home and find Simon – and some dinner!' she said. 'Race you!'

Seven

Simon was an enthusiast too. Once he'd heard their story, he agreed to keep a look out for Mr Bonser.

'While Mrs Hope shows him how to look after the dog, I'll make a rubbing from the front tyre,' he said. 'Then you can match it against your casts.' He winked at Mandy and slipped on his white coat, ready for surgery. 'You can rely on me,' he promised.

So the next day, Mandy skipped into the kitchen for breakfast, feeling delighted with herself. Everything was going to plan. She had the plaster casts, Simon was going to make rubbings of the tyres and James had the registration number of the van. All they had to do was to put the lot together and that would be the end of the badger-digging. And if Mr Bonser had left Patch to be attacked, well, that might just be the end of his dog-owning career. Humming happily to herself, Mandy shook a huge heap of cornflakes into her bowl.

And then the phone rang.

'It's for you!' Dad called, on his way through the hall. 'It's James.'

Good! thought Mandy as she picked up the receiver. James must have some important news about Mr Bonser, at last.

'Mandy, he's got away!' She could hear James's voice trembling even over the phone.

Mandy's thoughts were still on Mr Bonser. 'What do you mean?' she asked eagerly. 'Where to?' If Mr Bonser had disappeared, perhaps he'd warned the badger-diggers off and both Humbug and Patch would be safe.

'I don't know – I just heard from your grandad. I'll meet you down there – right away!' And James banged the phone down.

For a moment Mandy didn't move. It was a well-known fact that you couldn't do anything secret in Welford, but how on earth had Grandad heard about their visit to Mr Bonser? Mandy shivered: she had a feeling there was trouble about, though she couldn't quite work out what. Well, she'd better get over to Lilac Cottage straight away.

She took the short cut, over the back lawn, through the hedge and down the narrow path to the back garden of Lilac Cottage, practising the route to take on mornings before school the following week, since Humbug would need feeding.

Humbug! Mandy stood quite still in the middle of the path. Suddenly James's message made sense; it wasn't Mr Bonser who'd escaped. It was Humbug! That's why Grandad had rung James. The badger had got out and was on the loose – maybe going back to Piper's Wood.

With new-found energy she tore down the path, vaulted over the gate and raced across her grandparents' garden. James was already at the basement, his ear pressed to the door, listening intently.

'James!' Mandy ran up to him. 'What's happened?'

'Shh!' He just waggled a hand to her. 'Listen!'

Mandy pressed her ear to the door; she heard

only her own breathing, being rather puffed out after her run. There was no other sound.

'I can't hear anything,' she whispered.

'No, he's probably sleeping now.' James moved off, away from the basement, beckoning Mandy to follow him round the side of the cottage, to the kitchen door.

'Your gran's in quite a state,' he warned her.

She certainly was!

'He was up half the night rampaging about,' she told them. 'I thought we had burglars . . . Tom would insist on going down . . . it was quite frightening until we realised it was all that badger's fault.'

And James explained that Humbug had escaped from the hutch during the night, and gone hunting in the basement.

Mandy breathed a sigh of relief. 'Well, he must still be in there,' she said. 'We've only got to find him and put him back.'

But James shook his head doubtfully, looking rather gloomily at Mandy's grandmother.

Anyone could see she was quite upset, and Mandy couldn't blame her. She hadn't been happy about having the badger in the house from the start.

Mandy moved over to hug her grandmother. 'We'll make sure he's locked up safely when we get him,' she promised. 'It won't happen again.'

'It certainly won't,' said Gran. 'He's just got to go!'

Mandy decided this was not the time to argue. 'Where's Grandad?' she asked.

'He's looking for the key to the basement door.'

'No!' James almost shouted. 'We can't go in that way. As soon as the door's opened, Humbug'll be off like a shot across the garden.'

Gran shook her head. 'There's another door into the basement, from the hall. Even if the animal does escape it'll only get as far as the hall and you can catch him easily.'

As soon as Grandad came in with the key, they left Gran shut firmly in the kitchen with the kitten and went into the hall. Mr Hope unlocked the little door to the basement and Mandy and James stood by to catch whatever came rushing out.

But nothing did. The door creaked open but all was quiet. Very quickly, James led the way down the steps. Mandy followed and Grandad pulled the door shut as he came in last.

Only the sound of their breathing and the boiler hissing gently to itself disturbed the utter silence.

They stood still until their eyes became accustomed to the darkness, then they began to look around them. Mandy moved over to the hutch. Its door was still closed but even in that dim light she could see where the mesh had frayed away from the front. Humbug had obviously found a weak spot in the old wire and worked away at it.

'He's chewed his way out,' she whispered. 'He must have been desperate.' She thought of the little cub trying to get back to his home in the woods, and to his family who no longer lived there. Mandy sniffed loudly.

'Shh!' James hissed. But nothing stirred.

Grandad spoke very gently. 'I don't think we'll disturb him. Badgers are night-time creatures and he's been up and about for many hours. He'll sleep now, all day, I shouldn't wonder.'

'But where is he?' James was prowling about the dimly-lit basement, peering into corners, even up on shelves.

'He could be anywhere,' said Mr Hope. They all looked around the junk-filled basement. There were so many places for a small animal to curl up in: rolls of carpet, cardboard boxes, piles of gardening magazines, rows of paint tins, even the base of a spare bed propped against a wall. Where could they start looking?

'We'll have to wait until he's hungry and comes out,' said James. 'And keep watch.'

'But he might be asleep all day!' protested Mandy, forgetting to keep her voice quiet.

'Shh!' her grandfather reminded her. 'We'll take turns, and put food down, so that when he does wake he'll stop to eat.'

Lucky Humbug, thought Mandy, feeling suddenly hungry herself. She remembered her uneaten bowl of cornflakes on the breakfast table, and all the things she had meant to do that morning: feed her rabbits, clean them out, check up on the patients in the hospital, call to see Patch . . .

Suddenly struck by an idea, Mandy spoke out loud. 'Patch!' she said, 'that's who we need.'

'Mandy!' James whispered. 'If you can't be quiet go and do something useful.'

'Right!' said Mandy. 'You just hang on in here. I'll be back very soon.'

She ran lightly up the steps, slipped back through the hall door and was off home in a flash.

When she returned she brought a flask of coffee,

a bag of buttered scones – and Patch! Getting the coffee and scones had proved much easier than getting the dog.

'You can't take a dog out without the owner's permission,' Mrs Hope had told her when Mandy had asked to borrow Patch. 'You know Dad's rules.' But she had made a flask of coffee and buttered the scones for the badger watchers.

'Good luck,' she said 'I do hope you find the little badger. But don't go bothering Gran.'

When Mandy appealed to Simon, however, he agreed that a lost badger cub was more important than broken rules.

'But for heaven's sake have her back before the end of surgery,' he said. 'Whether you find the badger or not – right?'

'Right,' Mandy had promised.

Simon checked Patch's leg plaster, put on a collar and a lead, and told Mandy to carry the dog round to Lilac Cottage.

'She can walk about the basement, but that's all,' he said. 'Give her time to get used to the place before you put her down. Keep her on the lead. And as soon as that badger moves pick the dog up quick! We don't want any more wounds!'

* * *

James was horrified at the idea of setting the sharp little terrier to sniff Humbug out, but Mr Hope agreed with Mandy – it was the best way to find Humbug quickly. So he found a piece of old blanket and brought out the travelling cage.

'As soon as the badger moves out, you throw the blanket over him, Mandy picks up the dog, and I'll hold the cage. James, you pop him in, and there we are. Right?'

The other two nodded. Even in the dim light of the basement, Mandy could see James's white, tense face. She could feel Patch shivering in her arms, and for a moment she wondered whether they were doing the right thing. What if Patch set upon Humbug? And what if Humbug fought back? Poor Patch had suffered enough wounds from some fight or other.

But Patch made the first move, wriggling in Mandy's arms. Gripping the lead hard, Mandy carefully lowered the dog to the ground and followed her. The first thing she did was to squat on the concrete floor and make a puddle!

'Oh, dear, I'm so sorry, Grandad!' murmured Mandy. 'I'll scrub the floor when all this is over.'

Grandad smiled. 'She's just establishing her

territory,' he said. 'It may even be useful if Humbug gets the scent.'

But, wherever he was, Humbug was not getting any sort of scent. Patch hopped around happily, sniffing the walls and stopping for a long time to breathe in the fresh air from under the garden door. She obviously would have preferred her first outing to have been out there!

'Take her over to the hutch,' James suggested. 'Then she'll get Humbug's scent.'

'That might frighten her,' said Mandy. 'Don't forget what some wild creature did to her.'

'You can always give her one of your cuddles,' grinned James. He was feeling happier now he'd had some food, and now that there was some hope of finding Humbug soon.

Mr Hope put the old hutch down on the floor and Mandy gently led Patch towards it. As soon as the dog sniffed the straw, she backed off, snarling, hackles raised, eyes wild. And as if that was some sort of signal, there came a shuffling from a dark corner of the room.

Patch turned her head, nose quivering, tail vertical, and faced Humbug, who was advancing towards his hutch. For one moment they eyed each other, lean bodies stretched and still, both

shivering. Then with a savage cry, Humbug threw himself across the floor!

Quick as a flash, Mandy bent and picked up the terrier, holding her close in her arms and stroking her head. James, meantime, threw the old blanket over Humbug and held him close, well-wrapped but still struggling. Mr Hope held the travelling cage and James shoved Humbug in, blanket and all. Snap! The door was clipped down, the cage put up on the shelf and that was that.

The three of them grinned at one another. Now all they had to do was to face Gran.

* * *

'I'm sorry, Mandy, but I can't take another night like last night.' Gran pushed a mug of hot chocolate across the kitchen table. 'That animal has to go.'

James sipped his chocolate and looked gloomy. Mandy's grandfather nibbled a digestive biscuit thoughtfully.

'But it won't be another night like last night, Gran!' said Mandy. 'We'll get another hutch – a good one, one that Humbug can't escape from. He'll be quite safe.' She had no idea where they'd find another hutch; that was just the next problem.

'That's as may be, but have you thought why the little creature was trying to escape?' Gran looked round the table.

'He wanted to go hunting,' said James.

'He wanted to go home,' said Mrs Hope.

There was a silence. They all realised the truth of this. But how could they set Humbug free to live alone in a sett that had already been dug out?

'He hasn't got a home,' said James, sadly. 'And he hasn't got a family to look after him.'

Mandy sniffed. She turned her head away and looked across the kitchen. Quite worn out by her morning's work, Patch had settled herself in the kitten's basket by the cooker; the kitten was snuggled on her back, fast asleep.

'Look at that,' Mandy said. 'Humbug's only a kitten, too, you know, Gran. You wouldn't want to turn Smoky out, now would you?'

Gran shook her head slowly. 'But a badger is a wild animal,' she said quietly.

'And Humbug will go back to the woods as soon as we can arrange it,' said James.

'As soon as this afternoon?' Gran asked him.

And James shook his head.

Mr Hope stood up. 'Talking about this afternoon,' he said, looking over to his wife, 'hadn't we better be getting on with the packing?'

'Well, I don't know about that,' said Mandy's grandmother. 'Not after all this upset.'

'We were planning a trip in the camper van,' Mr Hope explained. 'Just a day or two, to get Smoky used to it.'

'But he's had enough excitement for one weekend,' said Gran. 'And so have I!'

Mr Hope smiled at her. 'Now look at that kitten,' he said. 'He'll be ready for anything after a rest. Just like you,' he added.

Mrs Hope laughed. 'Well, they say a change is as good as a rest, Tom.'

'So you'll come?' he asked her.

She nodded. 'Of course we'll have to take the cat basket and the travelling box, and several tins of cat food and . . .' She got up, ready to bustle away.

Mandy suddenly realised what her grandfather was doing. 'But Gran, if you're away this weekend, Humbug won't disturb you, will he?'

Gran stood still, looked at Mandy, then over to Mr Hope. 'Well, I suppose you've done it again, you two,' she smiled. 'I can't complain about being disturbed if I'm a hundred miles away, can I?'

Mandy grinned at James. James beamed over his glasses at Mrs Hope.

'Oh, thank you,' he said. 'I'll make sure he's quite secure this time.'

'And you must make sure you start preparing to let him go,' said Mr Hope. 'Dorothy's right, you know. He is pining for the woods.'

James nodded. 'I'll go and see Walter Pickard and get some advice. We'll set him loose quite soon,' he promised.

'Right! Now if we're to set off at all today, we must get on, Tom.' Mrs Hope started to collect the mugs.

'Oh, I'll clear up,' Mandy jumped up. 'Come on, James. I'll wash, you dry.'

Mr Hope looked down at the cat basket. 'I think you'd better get this dog back to Animal Ark,' he reminded her. 'And ask our Adam to bring a secure hutch round, too.'

A few minutes later, Mandy walked down the lane to Animal Ark, Patch snuggled in her arms. Back at Lilac Cottage, Humbug was snuggled in his mended cage, and everything was all right once more. She started to sing a lullaby to Patch as she made her way up the path to the red door of Animal Ark.

But she didn't finish the song. She stood in the middle of the path and looked at the van, parked right in the middle of the surgery carpark. A shabby, blue van.

Mr Bonser had taken her at her word. He'd come to collect his dog!

Eight

Mandy hesitated. No one had seen her; she could just turn round and run away with Patch. For a moment she even believed it. And then she came to her senses. Patch still had her plaster on, still needed treatment, and Mandy would never deprive her of that. Sighing, she walked slowly towards the surgery.

'Psst! Mandy – over here!'

It was Simon's voice. But there was no sign of Simon.

'Where are you?' she asked, quietly.

'Other side of the van – quick, before anyone sees you!'

Mandy slid round the back of the van and round the other side, hidden from the surgery. She heard a strange, rustling sound down by the near-side wheel. Looking down, she saw Simon busily rubbing a bit of wax crayon up and down on a paper pressed to the tyre.

'Where on earth have you been?' he asked without pausing. 'No, there's no time to tell me. Is the badger safe?'

Mandy nodded.

'Good. He's the only one who is.' Simon nodded up at the van. 'I had to tell your mum where the dog was, Mandy. I'm sorry. She's been trying to keep Mr Bonser busy in the office and Jean's been filling him with coffee and shortbreads. Go on – take the dog back up to the kennels.'

'We can't let him take her,' she protested.

'He may not even want her,' Simon pointed out. 'Not after all the instructions your mum's been giving him. But if he goes up to the kennels and finds her missing, he'll go berserk. Now – go!'

Obeying the urgency in his tone, Mandy walked round the front of the van, then slipped quickly past the surgery and round to the kennels. It took only a moment to put Patch into hers, click the lock and leave her standing there, alone and rather forlorn.

Even as Mandy turned to go she heard them approaching. Mr Bonser was talking in a very loud voice.

'You've no right,' he was saying. 'No right at all!'

Mrs Hope's face was serious, but she forced a smile.

'I really can't release a sick animal unless I'm sure you know how to take care of her,' she replied. 'Otherwise you must leave her with me for a few days.'

'I'll decide that, missus,' he said. 'Just let me see that dog.'

He strode down the path towards the kennels, then stopped when he saw Mandy. 'What are you doing 'ere?' he asked.

Mandy looked past him to her mother. She wasn't sure how to play this one. 'Oh, Mr Bonser,' she said in an over-sweet tone. 'I was just saying good morning to your little dog.'

He grunted and pushed past her. Mandy moved to stand by her mother, who, for some reason, pulled Mandy towards her and began brushing at the front of her old, black T-shirt.

'Oh, Mandy, when will you learn to eat your

cornflakes without them slopping all down you?'
she said.

Mandy was puzzled; she hadn't even had time
for breakfast that morning and anyway, she never
slopped it down her front. She looked down as
her mother frantically scrubbed at her front,
shifting Patch's white hairs.

'Oh!' said Mandy, with sudden realisation. She
glanced at Mr Bonser, crouching now in front of
the kennel. 'Oh, it's all right, Mum, it's only my
old T-shirt.' But she nodded to her mother and
mouthed her thanks.

'Come on out, you silly great dog!' Mr Bonser
was calling through the wire. He turned accusingly
to Mrs Hope. 'It's gone in,' he said. 'Won't come
out.'

And Mandy could just see a pair of little shiny
eyes peeping from the hut at the back of the run.

'Come on out,' he bellowed once more.

The dog merely lifted a lip in a snarl and
cowered back into the hut.

'You see, she's not ready to be taken out yet,'
Mrs Hope told him. 'She needs to rest a few more
days.'

But Mr Bonser shook his head, rather
desperately.

'I don't care what she needs,' he said. 'I need a dog.'

'Need?' Mrs Hope raised her eyebrows. 'What on earth could you need a little terrier like that for?' she asked.

There was a pause. Mr Bonser stood up, towering over both mother and daughter. 'Never you mind,' he muttered. 'That there's my dog and I'm taking it now!'

Mandy was puzzled; back at the farm, Mr Bonser had told her that the dog wasn't his but now he was claiming her as his own. She looked up at her mother, wondering whether to interfere. Better not, she decided. If anyone could face up to Mr Bonser, it was Emily Hope!

'Tell you what, Mr Bonser,' Mrs Hope spoke in a very reasonable tone. 'I'll keep the dog another day or two, just to keep an eye on her, at no extra cost to you. How does that strike you?' And she smiled her widest, most winning smile.

Mr Bonser stepped back, as if to ward off Emily Hope's charm. 'Strike me?' he said. 'It strikes me that you're kidnapping my dog!'

'Not at all, Mr Bonser,' Mrs Hope said coldly. 'I'm treating your dog for some rather unusual injuries.' There was no mistaking the threat in her voice.

Mr Bonser heard it. 'What do you mean?' he blustered.

'I mean that the dog has been badly treated: it's been in a very nasty fight with some animal or other but a healthy dog – a well-fed dog – would have recovered by now.' She drew herself up as tall as Bonser and looked him straight in the eye. 'In view of her general condition, I can't remove the plaster from her leg for a few days yet.'

Mr Bonser scowled. 'She can manage on three legs, can't she?'

Mrs Hope sighed. 'Yes,' she said. 'She can manage to hobble around, but she's not yet fit to go out. You can see for yourself she's still shocked and nervous.'

'No, I can't. Damned animal won't budge!'

Mrs Hope turned to Mandy. 'Could you persuade the dog to come out?' she asked, calmly.

Horrified, Mandy dropped her mother's hand and stepped back. Was she really going to hand Patch over to this man? But Mrs Hope merely nodded and urged her forward. With shaking fingers, Mandy clicked open the wire door and walked across to the hut.

'Patch!' she called, softly. 'Come on, Patch.'

She put her hand into the hut and tickled the

dog's ears. Patch licked her fingers and whined gently.

'Come on,' she murmured. 'I won't let him hurt you.' And she lifted the little terrier out.

'Well done, darling,' called her mother. 'Now, put her down on the ground, will you?'

Puzzled, Mandy knelt and put Patch gently on to the concrete floor. Immediately she hobbled back into Mandy's lap. Mandy looked back at her mother.

'Put her down again,' she said.

Mandy lifted the dog off her lap and gently put her on the ground. Patch looked round and hobbled a few steps. Then she caught sight of Mr Bonser and crouched on the concrete, shivering and snarling. Finally she turned and made a dive for Mandy's lap, pushed her muzzle right under Mandy's arm and hid her face, whimpering.

Mrs Hope turned to Mr Bonser. 'You see,' she said, gently. 'It's not only the physical wounds that have to heal. You must admit she's in no fit state to come back to work for you.'

'Who said anything about work?' he asked, suspiciously.

'You did. You said you needed a dog; I assumed you meant for ratting, or something . . .' Her words hung heavily between them.

Cuddling the terrified dog, Mandy looked in wonderment from Mr Bonser to her mother.

Suddenly the man turned. 'Tell you this much, missus,' he shouted. 'I'll leave it till tomorrow and if you don't release that dog then, I'll have the law on you.'

He pushed her roughly aside, strode down the path and jumped into his van. The ignition coughed several times before the engine started. Mandy hoped Simon had finished the tyre rubbings!

But Mr Bonser wasn't leaving yet. He thrust his head out of the van window. 'And you'll not get a penny off me!' He shouted. 'Not ever!' He revved the engine noisily, turned the lumbering vehicle round with a screech of tyres and shot down the drive, fast.

'Well, well, well,' murmured Mrs Hope. 'That was all rather interesting, wasn't it?' Suddenly she turned to Mandy. 'Right,' she ordered, briskly. 'Just leave the dog there, and let's go into the office. I think we need a little talk, don't you?'

Mandy hurriedly popped Patch back into the hut and followed her mother down the path between the kennels. She didn't like her mother's tone; there was going to be trouble right enough, and she was going to be in the middle of it! As they crossed the yard, the Land-rover pulled in, and Mr Hope dropped down from the driving seat, followed by James.

'Any chance of lunch for two hungry badger-tamers?' asked Mr Hope.

'Could you wait a moment, please, Adam?' Mrs Hope asked him. 'Come and join us in the office.' She looked straight at him. 'Mandy has something to tell us, I think,' she said.

Mr Hope looked across at Mandy and raised his eyebrows. Mandy miserably shook her head and plodded into reception, where Simon was standing at Jean's desk, apparently cutting out patterns with her scissors.

'Ah, Mandy!' he said. 'I think we've . . .' He paused as he watched Emily and Adam Hope striding past. Mandy didn't even look up. Only James, catching a glimpse of the papers in Simon's hand, stood back and pushed him on towards the office.

Emily Hope sat alongside her husband behind their desk. 'Do we really need *everyone* here?' she asked Mandy.

Mandy, who felt she needed all the support she could get just then, nodded.

'Right, well, you'd better sit down, then.' She nodded at Simon and James, who squashed down together on the one visitor's chair. Mandy remained where she was, standing in front of the desk, feeling she was about to be interrogated.

But Mrs Hope spoke in a quiet, calm voice. 'Now, Mandy, I think you've a few things to tell us. Like why Mr Bonser caught you up at his farm the other day, for instance.'

So Mandy took a deep breath, threw a desperate glance at her father, and told all. She explained how James and she had gone up to Old Dyke Farm to try to talk to Mr Bonser about the dog. And, she admitted, to take a closer look round his farm.

'It was my fault we went to the farm, Mum, so please don't blame James. He only took the registration number. And Simon's made rubbings of Mr Bonser's tyres today, to check against the plaster casts we made up in the woods. We're going to check on all the local vans if we can.' She paused to glance at her father, who smiled encouragingly.

'But what for, Mandy?' asked her mother.

'Well, if we can stop the badger-digging altogether, Humbug can go back home,' Mandy explained. 'Can't he, James?'

James nodded. 'Walter says there's a chance that the family will come back, if they're left alone,' he said. 'They often move to a kind of sub-sett, then return when they feel it's safe.'

'I can understand that you want to reunite Humbug with his family,' Mrs Hope smiled. 'But I don't see what Mr Bonser has to do with that.'

'Well . . .' Mandy took a deep breath and rushed on. 'I heard dogs whining in the piggeries at Old Dyke Farm. I think Mr Bonser is keeping them half-starved and hungry especially for digging badgers. I think we should do something about it!'

It was so quiet in the crowded office that Mandy could hear her own heart thudding, and James's nervous breathing just behind her.

'Well, you're right about the way he keeps the dogs,' said Mr Hope. 'I wasn't at all happy about the dog's condition when Mr Bonser first brought it in.'

Mrs Hope nodded. 'It wasn't only injured,' she agreed. 'It was half-starved.'

'You see, Mandy, we'd already decided to call in the RSPCA inspector to discuss the matter before contacting Mr Bonser,' Mr Hope explained.

'As it was, Mr Bonser got here first and flew at me!' Even Emily Hope sounded a bit shaken at the memory of her interview with Mr Bonser.

Mandy felt suitably ashamed. 'I'm really sorry, Mum,' she said. 'I never dreamed he'd come over so soon; he didn't seem to care what happened to Patch.'

'Yet he said he needed the dog for something this weekend,' mused Mrs Hope. 'I wonder why?'

'I don't think this has anything to do with protecting his land,' said her husband, grimly. 'I've heard a few rumours on my rounds. I didn't take much notice of them then, just gossip, you know, but Walter Pickard swears something's going on up in the woods this weekend . . .' And he went on to tell them how Walter had heard the men talking about a meeting on Saturday, and something about dogs and a great deal of money.

'I thought they must have been talking about racing greyhounds up at the track in Brudderford,' said Mr Hope. 'But it occurs to me now that it wasn't racing they were discussing at all . . .' He paused and looked round the office. All eyes were on him, James and Mandy looking very puzzled, Mrs Hope and Simon nodding thoughtfully. 'It's much worse than that,' he said.

'I'm afraid they were setting up badger-baiting.'

There was a stunned pause.

'You mean fights?' asked Mandy, in a wobbly voice.

Mr Hope sighed. 'They dig out the badgers, take them off to an old barn somewhere and set their dogs on them. They make bets on which one will win. Ernie Bell tells me it used to be a popular local sport.'

'But surely it's illegal?' said Mrs Hope.

'Of course it's illegal. And cruel. And disgusting.' Mr Hope reached for the telephone. 'And Mandy's right,' he said. 'We've got to do something – and fast!'

Nine

Mandy was not pleased. She'd been all set to dial 999 to get the Walton police station but Mr Hope wouldn't let her. 'Animals first' was his motto; he rang the Walton RSPCA. And now, after all the excitement there was nothing left to do except wait – and watch the rabbits run around the lawn.

Mandy sat on top of the empty hutch, kicking her heels. 'He should have let me ring the police,' she complained. 'What can the RSPCA do about Mr Bonser and his nasty friends?'

'Well, they're used to dealing with animals,' James joked.

But Mandy was in no mood for laughs. 'That's

just it,' she went on. 'They might well rescue the badgers – and the dogs – but in the meantime those . . . those . . . horrible people will be getting away.' Her voice choked. 'We ought to be keeping an eye on them, tracking them down – anything!' Mandy looked around impatiently, as if she'd like to arrest even the rabbits.

'But, Mandy, your dad said they're dangerous men – probably violent!' James shuddered.

He was right and Mandy knew it. Even so, she wished there was someone who would make sure that Mr Bonser and his friends didn't get away. But who?

'Dad said he'd heard rumours about the badger-baiters from Walter Pickard,' she said, thoughtfully.

'Well, Walter always knows what's going on in the woods,' said James. 'That's why he's our secretary.'

'Your secretary?'

'At the Welford Wildlifers,' James explained. 'Mrs Jackson is in charge, but Walter arranges the meetings.'

Mandy suddenly stood up and smiled. 'Well, maybe we'd better pay a visit to our friend Walter,' she said. 'Come on, let's get the rabbits in.'

* * *

'Well, well, if it isn't young James!' Walter was in his garden, sweeping up piles of leaves. 'And young miss with you, as well. New member is she?'

Blushing furiously, James shook his head.

'We just came to talk to you, Mr Pickard,' Mandy explained.

The big man pushed back his flat cap and peered down at Mandy and James. 'What can I do for you?' he asked.

'Well . . .' Mandy looked over her shoulder towards the garden gate. 'May we sit on your bench?' she asked. No point in the whole street hearing.

'Aye – come along with me, it's warm enough to sit out today.' Walter led the way and the three of them squashed together on the bench by the back door. As soon as they were settled, Walter's three cats came out to sit in the pale, autumn sunshine with them. Mandy bent to stroke Scraps whilst she collected her thoughts.

'Mr Pickard,' she began, 'Dad said you'd heard rumours about something going on up in the woods.'

Walter sucked at his teeth and nodded. 'I have that, young miss,' he said, in his deep, Yorkshire voice. 'Up to no good, somebody is up there.'

'Do you know who?' asked James.

Walter looked sideways at them. 'It's not for me to say,' he said, cautiously. 'But I have my suspicions. I have that!'

Mandy looked at James. James looked at Mandy. This was going to be difficult; they didn't want to give away all their evidence to Walter, who loved a good gossip. On the other hand, they did want to arouse his interest.

'You know Humbug, the baby badger that James rescued from Piper's Wood?' Mandy began.

The old man nodded. 'Oh, aye,' he said. 'Keeping all right, is he?' He turned to James.

'Yes, he's all right,' James picked up Mandy's train of thought. 'But it's getting time to set him free again. You warned me that we couldn't keep him away from the sett for more than a week or two.'

'That's right, young James. I'm glad you're keeping that in mind.' Walter gazed up the garden path and nodded slowly. 'I'm reminded of that time when I were a lad. Ernie Bell – just a lad himself – brought a badger out. Reared it like a ferret, he did, in a cage at the bottom of their garden. But he kept it too long. It got that big!'

Walter stretched out his hands. 'Solid an' all, it were. We didn't know what to do with it . . .'

'That's just it, you see,' Mandy burst in. 'If we turn Humbug – that baby badger – loose, and the diggers are still around . . .'

'Aye. And more than diggers, I hear.' Walter's eyes gleamed.

'Well, what we were wondering . . . my dad's got the RSPCA inspector coming round this afternoon and we've got to be there to tell him about . . . about how we found the badger. But we heard there's going to be more digging and we think somebody ought to keep an eye . . .'

'Certainly!' Walter drew himself up. 'This is a job for the Wildlife Watch Committee. Mrs Jackson's away just now, but I'll go up to the post office and talk to McFarlane. We often take a walk up the woods of an afternoon. Don't you worry, youngsters, we'll keep our eyes open.'

'Oh, thank you, Mr Pickard.' Mandy beamed up at him.

'It's nothing, lass,' said the old man, standing stiff, but tall and upright on his garden path. 'I'd best be getting off to see McFarlane, then . . .'

'Yes and we'd best be getting off back to Animal Ark.' James nudged Mandy and they both stood up. 'Thanks again, Mr Pickard!'

Together they raced back up the village, past the Fox and Goose and along the lane to Animal Ark. Mandy turned in at the gate first, then stopped.

'Wait!' she commanded. 'Look at that!'

She pointed to the front of the house where her father was leaning casually against the Land-rover and chatting to a tall, red-faced man with a dark beard.

Mandy pulled James into the rhododendrons. 'That's him!' she hissed.

'Who?' he asked, peering out of the bushes.

'Get back!' Mandy urged him. 'Isn't that the man who was spying on us in the woods? You know, the day you made the plaster casts.'

'I don't know; I didn't see him.'

They crouched together in the bushes, peering down the path to the carpark.

'I'm sure that's him,' said Mandy. 'And he was curious to know what you were doing that day.'

'Well, I expect it did look a bit odd,' said James.

'Yes, but he seemed to be checking up on us,' Mandy replied. 'Blackie even growled at him.'

'Just protecting you, I expect,' smiled James.

'Yes,' said Mandy. 'Blackie knew he was up to no good.' She pushed the fronds of leaves aside to clear her view. 'I don't like it,' she said. 'He's talking to my dad.'

'He looks quite friendly,' observed James. 'Maybe he's a friend of your dad's.'

Mandy threw him a withering glance. 'A friend of Mr Bonser's, more like,' she said. 'He's just come to spy on us, or to pinch the evidence or . . .'

'Or to get the dog?' suggested James.

Mandy stared at him. 'You're right,' she said. 'Mr Bonser's sent him to get his dog – maybe even to pay his bill. And you know what Dad is . . .'

James smiled. He did know. Mr Hope was wonderful with animals but soft as a brush with people. When it came to dealing with Mr Bonser's lot he wouldn't stand a chance.

'And Mum's out on a farm call,' groaned Mandy. 'Come on, we'd better rescue Dad!'

They rushed down the drive but as they approached the house, they walked slowly, trying to look casual.

'Where on earth have you two been?' said Adam Hope. 'This gentleman's waiting to see you. And he's been telling me all kinds of interesting things about our Mr Bonser.'

'I'll bet he has,' Mandy whispered. 'Like how he loves dogs and protects badgers.' She nudged James forward and followed, slowly.

'Come on!' Mr Hope urged. 'Now then, Ted, this is my daughter, Mandy, and James Hunter, a friend of hers.' He beamed down at the two of them. Neither looked at the stranger.

'This is Mr Forrester,' Adam Hope went on. 'Our new RSPCA inspector from Walton.'

There was a pause. Mandy opened her mouth, but nothing came out.

'I think we've met, haven't we, Mandy?' Mr Forrester smiled. 'Up in Piper's Wood, a few days ago?'

Mandy merely nodded.

'I hear you did a good job up there,' the inspector went on, turning to James. 'And the badger's doing well?'

'I hope so,' said James. 'But I want to return him to the sett as soon as . . . as it's safe.'

Mr Forrester nodded. 'Well, from what I've seen, we should be able to make it safe, for your badger and for any others which come back.'

James's eyes lit up. 'You think they might come back?' he asked.

'I think they already have done,' said the

inspector. 'I've been keeping a careful watch on the sett, as you know.' He looked sideways at Mandy, who blushed. 'There are traces – tracks and droppings, but no sign of them having settled in yet.'

'But you think they will?' asked Mr Hope.

'If they're left in peace.'

Mandy suddenly woke up. 'Well, they won't be left in peace unless we do something about Mr Bonser,' she pointed out.

Mr Forrester smiled at her. 'You're right,' he said. 'So shall we go in now and examine the evidence?' He looked at Mr Hope.

'Yes, yes, of course.' Mr Hope searched all his pockets for the surgery keys and looked vaguely all round. 'Now, where . . . ?'

Mandy reached into the car, fished a set of keys from the glove compartment and handed them to her father.

'Thank you. Right then, off we go!' Mr Hope led the way, James followed, then Mr Forrester, and, last of all, very quiet and thoughtful, came Mandy.

'These are very good casts,' said Mr Forrester, holding them up and examining them carefully.

'Lucky I saw you making them that day, isn't it?'

'Why?' asked James.

'Well, our friend Bonser could always claim you took the casts some other time,' said Mr Forrester. 'It's always useful to have an official witness.'

James looked knowingly over his glasses at Mandy. Mandy nodded and smiled back at him. Well, James had been right about Mr Forrester after all! They both watched the inspector pick up the photographs of the injured terrier. He looked at them in surprise.

'Good heavens!' he exclaimed.

'She was in a mess,' Adam Hope agreed. 'You

can see how talk started about some wild cat up there.'

Mr Forrester went on looking closely at the photographs, nodding thoughtfully. 'I'd like to see this dog right now, if you wouldn't mind.'

'Of course! Mandy will take you up there. And I'll ring that wildlife officer at police headquarters. Sergeant Wilkins, you said his name was?'

Mr Forrester nodded. 'Walton 78357, that'll get you straight through to him.' He turned. 'Now then, Mandy, let's go and look at this dog, shall we?'

Mandy walked beside Mr Forrester with very mixed feelings. She felt foolish for having mistaken him for one of Mr Bonser's men but relieved that at last he was getting things moving. And then she felt worried for Patch. Why was the inspector so interested in the little dog? Was he going to punish her for digging out badgers?

Silently she clicked open the cage and called, 'Patch? Come on, girl, come to me.'

The little dog put her head out cautiously, sniffed the air and hobbled out towards Mandy.

'Paddy!' Mr Forrester suddenly spoke. 'It *is* you – I thought it was! Come on, Paddy, here lass.'

The dog hesitated, looking first at Mandy then

at Mr Forrester. Mandy glared at the man; what did he mean by calling the dog Paddy? Suddenly, as if finally making up her mind, the little dog trotted up to Mr Forrester, yelping happily, jumping up and pawing his trousers. Mr Forrester bent down and picked her up.

'Well, I'm blowed!' he said, beaming across at Mandy. 'I never thought to see this little tyke again.'

Mandy just stood, staring, thoughts whirling round her head. 'Paddy', not 'Patch'. And the dog had chosen to run to Mr Forrester, not her. But how on earth did Patch know him?

The dog was wriggling in the man's arms, nuzzling up to his shoulder and whimpering with joy. For a moment, Mandy felt jealous; but even she couldn't help smiling at the little dog's delight.

'You know her, then?' she asked.

Mr Forrester pushed the dog's nose away from his face and nodded. 'I should say so! She's Jess Hargreaves's new farm dog. He took her from our dogs' home a few months ago when she turned up as a stray. When the dog went missing, I thought she'd run back to wherever she'd come from, but Jess was convinced she'd been stolen.'

'Well, he was right,' Mandy pointed out.

'Aye, he was, that.' Mr Forrester looked grimly down at the dog. 'And when we catch up with that Bonser, I'll remember Jess's face, the night his Paddy never came home.' He sighed and hugged the dog close.

Mandy stood watching, feeling rather awkward. Another case of mistaken identity, she thought. Well, at least Paddy didn't belong to Mr Bonser. Mandy knew that Jess Hargreaves took good care of all the animals on his farm.

Mr Forrester put the dog down and she ran up to Mandy, who knelt down and fussed her.

'You'll not want to see her go,' observed Mr Forrester.

Mandy blushed. 'Well, so long as she's not going back to that Mr Bonser,' she said.

'No, she's going back where she belongs – to work on a farm. You should see her snapping and nipping at those cows; gets them to the milking parlour in record time, she does!'

'I can just imagine her doing a job like that,' smiled Mandy. And she told Mr Forrester how Paddy had sniffed out Humbug in the basement.

He laughed. 'Well, Jess will be that thrilled to get her back,' he said. 'I must ring him right away.'

'Come on back to the office,' said Mandy. 'You can use the phone there.' Together they put Paddy into her hut and left her to sleep off her excitement, whilst they went off to face theirs.

Sergeant Wilkins, Mr Forrester and Mr Hope sat in the office, talking about Wildlife Acts and Cruelty to Animals Acts as if they had months to spare. Mandy was bursting to hear their plans, but she and James were dispatched to the kitchen with Mrs Hope and a policewoman to make their statements.

The policewoman made it all quite easy for them. She didn't ask them questions, but just let them tell her everything, right from the beginning, into a tape recorder.

'May I go back, now?' asked James.

The policewoman nodded. 'Want a lift home?' she offered.

'No thanks, I have to see to Humbug first,' said James.

'Ah, yes, the badger you rescued. Mind if I come and look at him?'

James looked doubtful. 'He's had rather a disturbing day,' he said.

'Oh, I'll be very quiet,' she assured him. 'I've

been a badger watcher for years. Do you have a badger watch in Welford?'

'No, but we could start one with the Wildlifers.' James smiled happily, and led her off, chatting all the time about badger problems. Mandy silently watched them go across the garden to the path to Lilac Cottage.

'Aren't you going with them?' asked her mother.

Mandy tossed her head and sniffed.

'What's the point in taking care of Humbug?' she asked. 'At this rate, there won't be anywhere safe for him to go back to!'

'What do you mean?'

'Well, there's Dad and the others all chatting away in the office, and James and that policewoman chatting away in the garden, and nobody's doing anything about catching Mr Bonser.' Mandy was impatient to get something done.

Her mother sat down next to her and put an arm round her. 'Don't be so impatient, Mandy,' she said. 'The police and the RSPCA are planning to catch Bonser red-handed tonight.'

'Tonight?' repeated Mandy, dismayed. 'But why leave it till then? Why don't they just go and arrest them right now?'

Mrs Hope shook her head. 'They've got to catch them at it,' she explained. 'Remember what Walter overheard? The next badger-digging will be this evening up in Darley Woods. And that's where they'll be caught.'

Mandy sniffed. 'But what about "animals first"?' she asked. 'We can't risk another injured dog, or badger even.'

'And we won't,' her mother promised. 'The police and the RSPCA inspectors will pounce before the dogs are even loose. There'll be no badger-baiting tonight.'

'Only Bonser-baiting?' Mandy smiled a wobbly smile.

Mrs Hope smiled back. 'That's right, Mandy,' she said. 'Now, how about taking some tea into the centre of operations?'

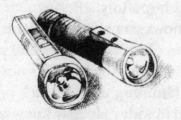

Ten

'It's not fair!' Mandy said to James as they went off to feed Humbug.

It had never occurred to her that she wouldn't be there to see Mr Bonser arrested. But Dad was quite firm; he would go along to check the dogs; the police and Ted Forrester's RSPCA team would do the rest. Children were not allowed!

'But we did all the work!' she said. 'We collected all the evidence, and now they won't even let us watch them catch him! Typical!' She slammed a tin of vitamin mixture down on the shelf.

'Shh!' James warned her.

He needn't have bothered. Stirred by Mandy's

voice, Humbug stretched up at the bars of his cage and snuffled hopefully.

'See, he knows you now,' said James.

Mandy forgot her bad temper and pushed a finger through to stroke the badger's nose. Assuming it was food, Humbug tried to suck on it.

'Ow!' cried Mandy. 'He may know my voice, but he doesn't know a finger from a pellet!'

James laughed. 'We've got to take him back to the sett once Mr Bonser's safely out of the way,' he said.

Mandy said nothing. Suddenly she felt quite left out; there was nothing for her to do. Not only was she going to miss all the action up in Darley Woods tonight, but she'd lost Patch! As soon as Jess Hargreaves had heard the news he'd come straight down to Animal Ark to collect his dog.

Sighing, she pressed the plastic lid on Humbug's pellet box and wandered back across the garden to Animal Ark. There was nothing much to look forward to now except school, she thought.

At six o'clock that evening, Adam Hope drove off in the Land-rover up to Darley Woods, to meet Ted Forrester, Sergeant Wilkins and their wildlife teams.

'Everybody's going to be there except me,' Mandy grumbled to her mother.

'And me,' Mrs Hope smiled. 'Shall we have supper on a tray in front of the television?' she offered.

Mandy knew she was giving her a treat, to make up for missing all the excitement – and to keep her occupied until they got some news. 'Thanks, Mum, what shall we have?' she said.

'I thought we'd share a pizza.'

'Great! And I'll mix the salad.' Mandy rushed off to the kitchen, relieved to have something to do to pass the time until her father came home.

But during supper, she couldn't relax. She hardly noticed what was on television, and only nibbled at her pizza.

'Come on, Mandy, it's no use worrying. Dad'll be all right,' said her mother.

'I know he will.' Mandy suddenly felt rather ashamed; she hadn't even been worrying about her father. 'I'm just sorry I won't be there to see it all through to the end.'

'I know, love, but these are dangerous men. You couldn't do anything even if you were there.'

'I could watch from a distance, couldn't I?'

Emily Hope looked at her daughter's sad face

and smiled. 'Honestly, darling, don't you think they'll have enough to do without looking after you?'

'I wouldn't need looking after,' Mandy assured her.

'No, perhaps not,' her mother agreed. 'But Dad'll be able to concentrate better without you there.'

And Mandy had to agree with that. She turned her attention to the hospital series on television and was soon engrossed.

She was so gripped by the programme that she didn't even hear the doorbell. Mum went off to answer it and came back with a worried-looking Walter Pickard.

' . . . so you see, missus, I thought I should come and tell Mr Hope 'cause he'd know what to do.'

Mandy turned off the television and looked at Walter's worried face. In spite of the blazing fire at her back, she suddenly felt cold.

'What is it?' she asked. 'Did you see something in the woods this afternoon?'

The old man shook his head. 'No, nothing happening up there today,' he said. 'Except we found traces of the badgers. I think they'll be ready to come back to their sett any time now if they're left in peace.' He turned to Mrs Hope. 'Then, Ernie Bell and me, we always goes for a game of dominoes at the Fox and Goose, early on, like. Good drop of ale they keeps there.'

'Yes, so I hear,' Mrs Hope smiled.

'But what has that to do with badgers?' asked Mandy, impatiently.

'What? Oh, aye. Well, it was very quiet about then, d'you see? And Ernie, well, takes a month of Sundays to decide which domino to play. So I'm just sitting there, waiting and sipping and . . . well . . . hearing . . .' Walter hesitated.

'And what did you hear?' Emily Hope prompted.

'It was from across t'other bar, you see? Two voices – sounded foreign to me . . .'

'Foreign?' Mandy asked, surprised.

'Aye, Lancashire maybe – or even up the Lakes somewhere. Anyway, they were talking about dogs and money and grumbling away about some meeting being changed . . .'

'Changed?' Mrs Hope's voice was suddenly anxious.

He nodded. 'Aye, changed from Darley Woods one chap said. Then the other asked him if he'd got a map, and first one said he didn't need it, he'd been up Piper's Wood before . . .'

'Piper's Wood!' both Mandy and her mother exclaimed.

'Aye, said as how they'd all meet up there . . .'

'When?' asked Mrs Hope, sharply.

Walter shrugged. 'I dunno,' he said. 'Ernie put his domino down just then and by the time I'd played him out they'd gone.'

'But you think they meant tonight?'

'Certain sure. That's why I wanted to tell Mr Hope, you see? Young James told me he was seeing the RSPCA chap and I thought . . .'

'Yes, yes, you were quite right, but they've all gone off to Darley Woods! Oh, what on earth should we do?' Emily Hope stood up and paced round the sitting-room, biting her lip anxiously.

Mandy stood up, too. 'We'll have to get a message over to them,' she cried. 'Let's call the police.'

That was only the start of Mandy's surprising evening. As soon as she'd passed the message on to the police station at Walton she rang James and told him to get ready for a badger watch.

'A what?' James couldn't believe his luck.

'Well, it's a Bonser watch really.' Mandy explained that Walter and her mum were going to keep an eye on things until the official party arrived. 'And I've persuaded Mum to let me come along this time. You will come, won't you?'

James hesitated. Watching badgers was one thing, but getting involved with Bonser and his crew . . . 'I don't know if they'll let me,' he said.

'Of course they will if you tell them you're with Mum. See you in ten minutes – be ready!' Mandy put down the phone and, smiling happily to herself, went in search of wellingtons.

'And you're to stay in the car no matter what happens, do you hear?' Mrs Hope told Mandy and

James. 'Walter and I will keep watch in the undergrowth closer to the sett. You lock the car and stay there. Right?'

'Right, Mum,' Mandy promised.

It was already quite dark in the woods but Mrs Hope didn't want to use the lights. Slowly, cautiously, she drove the car along the track where Mandy had found the tyre prints that day. It seemed like months ago, she realised now. But before she could comment, the two adults were out of the car and checking the doors.

'We're only keeping watch until the others arrive,' said Mum. 'Chances are, nothing will happen this part of the evening.'

'I hope she's wrong,' said Mandy. 'Don't you?'

'Hmm.' James didn't sound very sure.

He'd rather be watching for badgers than for badger-baiters, Mandy reflected. She waved to Walter, who gave a thumbs-up sign and followed Mrs Hope into the undergrowth.

And then it was very, very quiet. Mandy would never admit it, but she actually slept for a while. She was awakened by James gripping her arm.

'Look!' he whispered pointing across the clearing.

Mandy saw lights – torches – and heard people

pushing through the undergrowth. Then the sound of panting, snuffling, the occasional yelp. The dogs!

'What shall we do?' she whispered.

'Nothing – just watch,' said James.

'We'll get a better view at the front,' suggested Mandy.

She and James clambered into the front seats, watching the procession as it made its way to the clearing. The car was well hidden but even so, Mandy felt a shiver run right through her. Where was her mother? And Walter? And, more important, had Dad and the others got the message?

Pushing her worries away, Mandy concentrated on the scene before her. Several men now appeared in the lamplight, carrying ropes, spades, and some smaller tools Mandy didn't recognise. The dogs strained and tugged on the bits of rope that held them, sniffing and yelping, pulling the men closer and closer to the sett.

'I hope they don't get the scent of Walter or Mum,' whispered Mandy.

'Not Walter; he'll have the sense to stay upwind of them and your mum'll be with him.'

Just then a terrible sound hit the air. A scream,

a shriek, and a long, high howl that ended in a series of agonised yelps.

Mandy sat up still and straight. 'What's that?' she whispered.

James pushed his glasses up his nose and peered through the front window. 'I can't see,' he moaned. 'It's all misted up.'

'Wipe the windows – come on!' Mandy started rubbing at hers with her handkerchief.

James hesitated. 'I haven't got a hankie,' he said.

'Well, look in the glove compartment – there's usually a duster or something in there.'

James found the duster and wiped his window down then stood up to clean the whole of the front while Mandy peered out. In the bobbing lamplight she could just make out a circle of figures – the badger-baiters. Within the circle she saw two short, dark shadows shifting about each other then, suddenly, launching one on top of the other. And the screaming and the shrieking again.

Sickened, Mandy sank back in her seat. 'What shall we do? What shall we do?' she moaned, her face hidden in her hands.

James joined her; she could feel him trembling even through the car seat. 'They didn't even have to dig one out tonight,' he said, bitterly. 'That was probably Humbug's mother coming to look for him again.'

For a moment both of them sat, silent, shaking, looking nowhere, at nothing. Then suddenly the car was flooded with light.

'What's that?' Mandy lifted up her face and saw a dazzling light that filled the clearing. People were racing across the grass right into the circle of badger-baiters. Then howls and barks and thuds and curses.

Mandy and James stood up now and leaned forwards to the front window, trying to make sense of the scene. Police were certainly there – and Dad! Mandy could see his heavy figure crouched down by the pack of dogs and she knew he would be muzzling them.

As she strained forward to see more clearly, Mandy saw a figure pounding along the track towards them. One of them had got away! She cowered back as the figure hesitated in front of the car. What if he tried to get in? Mandy watched fearfully as he pushed past and pounded off down the bridle-path.

Then, something hit the roof with a clang. Mandy jumped, still afraid that someone might be trying to get in. But whatever it was slid down the back of the car and all was quiet again.

'What was that?' James jumped. He hadn't even seen the escaped man. 'It sounded as if somebody threw something at us,' he said.

That was it! Mandy realised. The man had thrown something over his shoulder as he ran away. But what could it have been? And whatever it was, he was keen to lose it.

She turned to tell James about him, but he was peering through the front window again.

'Here's your mum and Walter,' he said. 'It's all over.'

'You all right, you two?' Mrs Hope unlocked the front doors. 'See, you didn't miss out after all.' She smiled at the two of them, sitting quietly in the front seats. 'Hop into the back, then.'

As they scrambled out of the front of the car, Mandy nipped to the back. She could see nothing in the dark, but she caught the toe of her trainer on something hard. She bent down and picked up some sort of metal tool. It felt long and thin and swung in her hand, as if on a pivot. What on earth could it be?

'Come on, Mandy – get in quickly!' her mother urged her.

Shoving the tool up into her anorak sleeve, Mandy joined James in the back seat.

'Don't forget your belts,' Mrs Hope warned them.

Mandy groped around for her seat-belt. As her fingers connected with the metal buckle, she wondered just what she'd got up her sleeve. She was about to bring it out and tell them all about it but everyone else was busy talking.

'Was the badger hurt?' James was asking.

'Good heavens, no,' Mrs Hope reassured him. 'She was a real fighter. Now we know where Paddy got those wounds.'

Mandy remembered her first sight of the little terrier and shuddered. So her wounds could have been caused by one of Humbug's own family! 'What about the dog?' she asked.

'Mr Hope's bringing it back,' said Walter. 'The others are going to the dogs' home. They're a right wild pack and no mistake.'

'And the men?' asked James. 'What will happen to them?' Mandy knew he was hoping that Mr Bonser would be put out of the way so that Humbug could return to the sett.

But her mother didn't answer straight away.

'Well, they'll be charged, of course,' she said,

slowly. 'Probably for ill-treating the dogs, not the badgers. Trouble is, they claim they were digging out foxes. Mr Bonser says he hired them because the foxes have been at his poultry. Fox-digging has only recently been made illegal – everybody knows it still goes on.'

'Aye,' Walter went on. 'And everybody who's lost any chickens to a fox will agree with Bonser.'

'But surely no one will believe they were after foxes?' asked Mandy.

'What they believe and what they can prove are two different things,' said Walter. 'That's what they need – some real hard evidence.'

Mandy sat in the back of the car, feeling her arm stiff where the metal was still hidden up her sleeve. Was this 'real, hard evidence'? It felt a bit long and thin, with rounded bits that got caught in the lining of her sleeve. Well, it might be important, she thought. After all, that man had tried to get rid of it. But how could a bit of metal turn into crucial evidence? Mandy's thoughts whirled but she was too tired to make any sense of them just then.

I'll wait till Dad gets home, she promised herself. *He'll know what it's all about.* She yawned, put her head back on the seat and was almost asleep by the time they arrived at Animal Ark.

Eleven

It was just like a party in the kitchen at Animal Ark. Walter sat by the cooker drinking coffee with Ted Forrester, Mr and Mrs Hunter called to collect James and stayed on to hear all about the night's events, Adam Hope poured drinks and Emily Hope made a stack of sandwiches for everyone.

'Well, let's hope those men get put away for a very long time,' said Mrs Hunter.

'Oh, they'll claim they were only after foxes,' said Mr Hope, handing her a drink. 'They'll probably get away with a fine for that.'

'And they'll still be free to dig out our badgers!'

said Mrs Hunter. 'We'll have to keep a look out from now on.'

'You'd be at it twenty-four hours a day,' said Ted Forrester. 'And even then they'd find another sett in some other wood.'

Walter nodded in agreement. 'McFarlane's trying to get a badgerwatch started,' he said. 'But there's not enough Wildlifers to keep watch round the clock.'

Mandy put down her glass of Coke and looked across the table at James. He pushed a sandwich round his plate, making no attempt to eat it. She knew he was thinking about Humbug, worrying about setting him free with the baiters still on the loose . . .

'Well, the police will comb that clearing tomorrow,' Mr Hope was telling Mrs Hunter. 'They must have got rid of at least one pair of tongs.'

'Tongs? What do they use them for?' asked Mrs Hunter.

And across the table, Mandy was all ears.

'They use them to lift the badgers,' Adam Hope explained. 'To avoid those strong claws, you see.'

'And they'd only need them if they were after badgers, not foxes?' Mandy asked.

'Well, yes – they're a dead giveaway,' her father told her. 'But those men certainly hadn't got any with them tonight.'

'Oh, yes, they had,' said Mandy. 'Hang on!' She ran out to the hall and came back struggling with her anorak.

'What on earth . . . ?' asked Emily Hope. 'Do be careful, Mandy – you'll tear that sleeve.'

'There you are!' Mandy finally extricated the metal tongs from her anorak. She held them up for everyone to see. 'A man ran past our car while you and the police were all busy,' she explained. 'And he threw these behind him.'

'How did you find them?' asked Mrs Hope.

'I heard them clatter on the car roof and slide down the back,' said Mandy.

'That's right,' said James. 'We wondered what it was.'

'Then, when we got out of the car to change places,' Mandy explained, 'I looked round the back and just about fell over these things.'

'Well done, Mandy,' said Ted Forrester. 'Tongs are always accepted as vital evidence.'

'But what if the gang deny they were theirs?' asked Mr Hunter. 'Mandy's fingerprints must be all over them by now.'

Mandy looked round in dismay. After all that, she hadn't got any real, hard evidence! If only she'd left them for the police to pick up!

'Don't worry, Mandy,' her father reassured her. 'If the runaway man had any sense he'd already wiped them clean.'

Mandy smiled – a small, wan smile. She still felt disappointed that her evidence was not going to be as final as she'd hoped.

But Walter Pickard was speaking. 'Well, I'll bet them there tongs have got some mark or other on them, Mr Hope,' he said.

'What do you mean?'

'Well, country folk generally mark their tools, so that when other folk borrows 'em and never bring 'em back, they can prove who they belong to, see?'

'You mean the tongs will have a name on them?' Mandy asked.

'Nay, it won't be a name. More a sign, like.' Walter fiddled in his waistcoat pocket and brought out a pair of round, steel-rimmed glasses. 'Now, give them tongs to me,' he said to Mandy. 'Careful, now . . .' He took the tongs by one of the handles, holding it delicately in his broad fingers, and peered closely at the blades.

Everyone watched. No one spoke. The tongs spun round, catching the light. Suddenly Walter pointed to a mark scratched deep into the metal right on the joint of the two blades.

'Reckon that's a "B",' he said. 'You mark my words!'

Ted Forrester passed extra-strong peppermints to the other two with him in the hide. 'To keep you awake,' he said. 'I always use them when I'm keeping watch.'

'For badgers or criminals?' asked Mandy.

'Both,' he grinned.

'Shh!' said James, anxiously peering through the hide he and Walter had made earlier that day, before they set Humbug free.

Now it was nightfall and Ted Forrester had brought them on the first badger watch of the season. Mandy had never been keen on just watching animals; she preferred to be close enough to touch them. But now she was really excited. She sucked so hard on her mint that her eyes began to water. She shook her head and looked out into the moonlight to clear them. And as she peered out, she caught sight of a movement in the deep shadows under the trees. She peered more closely and saw it emerge into the moonlight – a badger.

But it wasn't Humbug. It was a larger, older animal which trotted out into the clearing so quickly that Mandy thought perhaps it was merely a shadow, a trick of the light.

But Ted had seen it too. 'A fully-grown male,' he whispered. 'See the length of him? And how black the markings are on his face? Females are lighter – in weight as well as colour; fatter, too.'

Mandy and James followed his gaze. The badger was certainly bigger than Mandy had ever imagined. He trotted out into the clearing, lifted up his dark snout and sniffed. They could even hear him!

'Now, don't get too excited; they often live alone, male badgers.'

Suddenly the badger stopped, sat down, and began to have a good scratch. Mandy could hear the rasping of his claws quite clearly, could see the sharp snout, lifted into the light. She felt a shiver of excitement; her first really wild badger! Even if Ted Forrester was right, and this was a solitary male, it was worth waiting for.

But Ted was wrong. As the first badger sat enjoying his scratch, another smaller but plumper

animal emerged into the light, closely pursued by two cubs!

'Young female – and cubs!' James sounded excited even in whispers.

Mandy held her breath. Was one of them Humbug?

But there was too much going on to worry about Humbug. First the male stopped scratching, sat up, and gently rolled the cubs around on the grass. Then he lay down and allowed the cubs to 'attack' him. It was so quiet that the badger watchers could hear the excited squeaks of the cubs as they rolled all over the male, and fell off his back, into the grass.

Suddenly, the female darted forward, grabbed a cub in both of her front paws, and began to groom it roughly, pushing and licking and patting it into shape. Satisfied, she let him go back to his game and grabbed the other one. This time she was gentler, coaxing, rather than forcing the little creature to stay still, licking him delicately, lovingly.

'That's Humbug!' breathed Mandy. 'She's being extra careful with him because she lost him once.'

'Might very well be,' Ted Forrester nodded. 'She's certainly taking extra care of that little 'un. I don't think we need to worry about Humbug any more,' said Ted Forrester. 'He's been accepted, all right.'

As if to prove him right, the smallest badger ran off squeaking into the shadows, pursued by the other cub and their mother. The male snuffled around in the grass, making his way into the undergrowth, slowly, steadily, and then he was gone.

So was the light; clouds covered the moon and the woods were suddenly quite dark.

'Time to go home, I think,' said Ted. And the three of them wriggled out of the hide, through the bracken, and ran down the track to his car.

'Brilliant!' declared Mandy from the back seat. 'That was one of my best nights ever.'

'Better than looking after sick animals even?' inquired James.

Mandy laughed. 'Of course it was,' she said. Better than checking the animals of Animal Ark or playing with her pet rabbit, she thought. Perhaps when she grew up she'd be a Wildlife Officer like Sergeant Wilkins, or an RSPCA inspector like Ted.

Mandy gazed dreamily into the gathering darkness until she saw the words 'Animal Ark' picked out by the headlights. She smiled. Perhaps she'd be a vet after all.

Lucy Daniels

KITTENS IN THE KITCHEN

Not everyone cares for animals as much as Mandy does. When a stray cat gives birth in Mr Williams's kitchen, he is absolutely furious. He has no sympathy for the mother, and wants nothing to do with the kittens – they have to go.

Can Mandy find homes for four newborn kittens in just one week?